wM 6/90 ¢ 11/23

W9-AZT-664

"I don't know why she appointed me, either."

The tension emanating from Slater as Chris made the admission startled her.

"Oh, come on, Chris," he said icily. "We both know *exactly* why Natalie chose you."

Slater turned on his heel and left her before she could say another word. The blow he'd just dealt her was severe. He knew! He knew how she felt about him and just why Natalie had appointed her co-guardian of her daughter. Slater knew, and he was adding to her torment deliberately. He must hate her nearly as much as Natalie had.

Instinctively she wanted to escape, to put as much distance between herself and Slater as she could. But she couldn't do it. For little Sophie's sake she had to stay....

Books by Penny Jordan

HARLEQUIN PRESENTS

HARLEQUIN SIGNATURE EDITION

These books may be available at your local bookseller.

Don't miss any of our special offers. Write to us at the following address for information on our newest releases.

Harlequin Reader Service
P.O. Box 52040, Phoenix, AZ 85072-2040
Canadian address: P.O. Box 2800, Postal Station A,
5170 Yonge St., Willowdale, Ont. M2N 6J3

PENNY JORDAN

you owe me

Harlequin Books

TORONTO • NEW YORK • LONDON
AMSTERDAM • PARIS • SYDNEY • HAMBURG
STOCKHOLM • ATHENS • TOKYO • MILAN

Harlequin Presents first edition November 1985
ISBN 0-373-10833-8

Original hardcover edition published in 1985
by Mills & Boon Limited

Copyright © 1985 by Penny Jordan. All rights reserved.
Philippine copyright 1985. Australian copyright 1985.
Except for use in any review, the reproduction or utilization of
this work in whole or in part in any form by any electronic,
mechanical or other means, now known or hereafter invented,
including xerography, photocopying and recording, or in any
information storage or retrieval system, is forbidden without
the permission of the publisher, Harlequin Enterprises Limited,
225 Duncan Mill Road, Don Mills, Ontario, Canada M3B 3K9.

All the characters in this book have no existence outside the
imagination of the author and have no relation whatsoever to
anyone bearing the same name or names. They are not even
distantly inspired by any individual known or unknown to the
author, and all the incidents are pure invention.

The Harlequin trademarks, consisting of the words
HARLEQUIN PRESENTS and the portrayal of a Harlequin,
are trademarks of Harlequin Enterprises Limited and are
registered in the Canada Trade Marks Office; the portrayal
of a Harlequin is registered in the United States Patent
and Trademark Office.

Printed in U.S.A.

CHAPTER ONE

THE letter caught up with Chris in New York. She had been working there for a month—one of her longest spells in one place in nearly six months—modelling clothes for one of New York's top designers and sandwiching between the shows photographic sessions under her five year contract with a large cosmetics house.

That was the trouble with getting to the top of the modelling profession, she thought wryly, as she let herself into the apartment she had 'borrowed' from an American model, for the duration of her assignments in New York—the work came thick and fast, but there wasn't enough time to do it all. She was twenty-six now; and she had promised herself when she took up modelling she would only stay in it four years. She had been twenty then. Grimacing faintly she bent automatically to retrieve the mail that had slipped from her fingers on to the floor. Her needs were not extravagant, but her aunt's final illness had been extremely expensive financially. The illness from which her aunt had suffered had been progressive and terminal involving mental as well as physical destruction, and Chris was only thankful that during those final few years her aunt had retreated into a world of her own where the true nature of her own decline was concealed from her. Two months ago her aunt had died, and although now there was no reason for her to continue earning large sums of money, Chris admitted mentally that it was too late for her to change her career. She could model for possibly another four years if she was lucky, and during that time she should earn enough to keep her in comparative comfort for the rest of her life—if she was careful. But what was she going to *do* with the rest of that life? Seven years ago she thought she had known exactly what course her life would take. Marriage to Slater; children. The smile curving her mouth was totally humourless. So much for dreams. Reality was a far cry from her late teenage hopes.

The midsummer heat of New York had darkened her honey-blonde hair slightly with perspiration. Thank God for air conditioning she reflected as she dropped the mail on the small coffee table and headed for the shower. Being able to lease Kelly Reading's apartment had been a welcome bonus on this assignment, she was tired of living out of suitcases; of moving from city to city, always the traveller. That was never how she had envisaged her life. It was strange really that she, the stay-at-home one, should have a career that made her travel so widely, whilst Natalie, her restless, will o' the wisp cousin should have been the one to marry, to have a child.

Frowning Chris stripped the silk suit from her body, the firm curving lines of it too familiar to her to warrant undue attention. In all her years of modelling she had always refused topless and nude shots. And received a good deal of heat from her first agent for it, she remembered wryly. Things were different now. As one of the world's top models she could pick and choose her assignments and Hedi, her agent, had clear instructions about what she would and would not accept.

As she stepped into the shower stall she swept her hair up into a loose knot. Long and honey-blonde, it was thick and resilient enough to adapt to the differing styles she had to adopt. She showered quickly and then stepped out, wrapping her body in a towel before starting to remove her make-up. As always when she had been wearing it for several hours she itched to be free of it. A model girl who hated make-up. She laughed derisively, cleaning eyeshadow from the lid of one sea-green eye. Her beauty lay in her bone structure and her eyes, and was ageless.

Her looks had always been a source of contention between them when she and Natalie were young. Orphaned at five she had been brought up by her aunt and uncle alongside their only child, Natalie, who was two years younger than Chris. Tiny, dainty Natalie, who she had soon learned, possessed a cruelly vindictive streak, which she used unmercifully to protect what she considered to be hers, and that had included her parents and all her friends. Chris had not found it easy to accept her unwanted role as 'orphan', and many times during those early days she had retreated to her bedroom to indulge in secret tears when Natalie had taunted her about her orphaned status. 'You would have had to go in a home if you hadn't come here,' had been one of Natalie's favourite taunts, often with the threat tagged on of '. . . and if I don't like you, you will still have to go there.'

Under that threat Chris had weakly, hating herself for her weakness, given in to many forms of blackmail, which ranged from the subtle never-expressed pressure from Natalie that she would always keep herself in the background, to open demands for 'loans' from Chris's pocket money.

Sighing Chris moisturised her skin. She could see now that Nat had just been insecure. There had been a bond between aunt and niece that had never truly existed between mother and daughter. Even in looks she had resembled her aunt, Chris acknowledged, and Natalie with the perception that most children possessed had sensed her mother's leaning towards her sister's child and had bitterly resented Chris for it.

Nat, on the other hand had always been her father's favourite. Uncle Robert had adored his small, dark-haired daughter, 'his little pixie fairy' as he had called her. His death in a road accident when Nat was fourteen had severely affected her. Funnily enough she herself had never shared Nat's deep resentment of their relationship, and as she had grown older she had adopted a protective instinct towards her younger cousin, knowing without anything being said that she was entering a conspiracy with her aunt which involved a constant feeding of Nat's ego; a never-ending soothing of her insecurities. As a child Nat had grown used to her father describing her as the 'prettier' of the two cousins, and with her dark curls and small, frail frame she had possessed a pretty delicacy that Chris lacked. When, as a teenager, Chris had started to blossom Natalie had been bitterly resentful.

'Boys hate tall girls,' she had told Chris spitefully. And Chris could still remember the occasion when, one very hot summer, she had been sent for by the Headmistress, because Nat had told her teacher that her cousin bleached her hair, strictly against the rules of the school. In point of fact, its extreme fairness that summer had been the result of more sunshine than usual, and when pressed for an explanation as to why her younger cousin should try to get her into trouble deliberately, Chris had leapt immediately to Natalie's defence. She could still remember her headmistress's words on that occasion.

'Chris, my dear,' she had told her firmly, 'your desire to protect Natalie is very natural and praiseworthy, but in the long run you would be helping her more if you allowed her to take responsibility for her actions. That's the only way we learn to think carefully before we commit them.'

Would life have been any different if she had heeded that advice? Grimacing, Chris extracted fresh underwear from the drawer. It took two to commit treachery; Natalie alone could not be blamed for the destruction of all her bright—and foolish—dreams.

It was another half-an-hour before she discovered the letter. She had just mixed herself a cooling fruit drink and sat down, when she caught sight of it, protruding ominously from among a stack of mail, the solicitor's name and address in one corner, the airmail sticker in the centre.

She had grown used to correspondence with Messrs Smith & Turner during the weeks following her aunt's death. On her marriage Natalie had deliberately, and to Chris's mind, quite heartlessly cut off all ties with her mother. 'She always loved you best,' she had told Chris spitefully, when she tried to talk to her about it. 'I never want to see her again.'

It had been a couple of years after that that Chris had actually noticed the oddness of her aunt's behaviour and another harrowing seven months before her condition had been correctly diagnosed. The specialist, sympathetic and understanding had told Chris of an excellent nursing home which specialised in such cases, and where her aunt would receive every kindness and the very best of care.

The fees had been astronomical. Chris had written to Natalie, believing that she would want to make her peace with her mother in view of her failing health, but Natalie had never even replied, and it had been more than Chris could have endured to go down to Little Martin and talk to her. In order to pay the nursing home fees she had committed herself to a gruelling number of assignments, and for the last four years she had barely had time to take a breath.

Now it was over, and she presumed the letter from Smith & Turner related to the final details surrounding her aunt's estate, if her few belongings and the house in Little Martin could be classed as that.

It had come as no surprise to Chris to discover that her aunt had left her the house. She had bought it after Uncle Roger's death, selling the larger property and investing the difference. Chris had always loved the thatched cottage, despite its many inconveniences, but Nat had hated it. She never forgave her mother for selling the larger property, and constantly complained about their drop in living standards. In anyone else Chris would have denounced her cousin's behaviour as brutally selfish, but because of her childhood conditioning Chris was constantly finding mental excuses for her. Although there was one sin she could never forgive her ... Idly sliding her nail under the sealed flap she extracted the sheets of paper inside.

Her heart thumped as she read the first line, barely taking in its message, her eyes racing back to the beginning and tracing the words once again. '... regret to inform you of the death of your cousin, Natalie James née Bolton, and would inform you that ...'

Without reading any further Chris lifted her eyes from the paper. Natalie dead! She couldn't believe it. She was only twenty-four. What had happened?

She glanced at the date on the letter and her heart dropped sickeningly. Natalie had been dead for six weeks! Six weeks, during which she had travelled from Nassau to Rio, then on to Cannes and finally to New York.

She dropped the letter on to the floor, filled with a mixture of nausea and guilt. How often during the last seven years had she wished Natalie out of existence? How often had she prayed that she might wake up and discover that what had happened was all just a nightmare? Only now could she admit to herself the frequency of such thoughts, generally after she had just had to point out to yet another male that being a model did not mean that she was also available as a bed mate. She had never wanted her present life; it had been thrust upon her in a manner of speaking; a means of salvaging her pride and her dignity, and also a means of . . . of what? Escaping her own pain?

No. Not entirely. Deep inside her had been the unacknowledged thought that by leaving somehow she was giving something to Natalie's unborn child—Slater's child. The child that should have been hers.

The doorbell rang and she slipped the intercom switch automatically, shocked out of her involvement with the past when she heard Danny's familiar New York accent.

'Danny, I'm not ready yet,' she apologised. In point of fact she had lost what little desire she had possessed to go out with the brash New Yorker, who had forced his way into her life three weeks ago. Tall, fair, good looking, and well aware of his attractions Danny had been chasing her from the moment of her arrival, and was, Chris was certain, supremely confident that in the end he would catch her. She, however, had other ideas. Charming though Danny was he couldn't touch the deep inner core she had learned to protect from the world. No man had touched that since Slater.

Ten minutes later she was down in the lobby with Danny, the poise she had learned over the years covering her innate inner turmoil.

They were dining out with a business associate of Danny's. He wanted to show her off like a child with a new and status-symbol toy, it was an attitude she had grown accustomed to.

They were to go to a chic, 'in' restaurant, which would be full of New York glitterati, and Chris's spirits sank as she got into the taxi. Natalie dead! Even now she could not take it in. What had happened? She wished now she had read the letter more fully, but she had been simply too stunned. She supposed it was natural that the solicitors should write to her as Natalie's closest blood relative after her daughter. She knew that Natalie had had a girl, her aunt had told her, wistfully, longing for an opportunity to see her only grandchild, but knowing it would be denied her.

If it hadn't been for Ray Thornton, she herself would have had to stay in Little Martin, enduring the sight of Natalie living with Slater as his wife. She had a lot to thank Ray for. Slater had never liked him. 'Flash' he had called him, and in a way it was true. Ray had made his money promoting pop stars. He had been thirty-one to Slater's twenty-five then, fresh from the London 'scene' and defiantly brash. She had liked him despite it, although then she had turned down the job he had offered her in the new club he was opening in London. She had then only known him a matter of months and yet he had been the one she had turned to that night, when she had discovered Natalie in Slater's arms. He had comforted her bracingly then, just as he had done when Natalie announced her pregnancy. It was Ray who had told her she ought to become a model. It was Ray who had introduced her to the principal of the very select London modelling school where she had trained. 'A little too old for a beginner' was how Madame had described her, but she had more than repaid Ray's faith in her. For a while he had pursued her, but only half-heartedly, recognising that she was still far too bruised to contemplate putting anyone else in Slater's place. They had kept in touch. Ray was married now and lived in

California. Chris liked his wife and he had the most adorable two-year-old son.

The evening dragged on interminably. Chris was aware of the sharp, almost disapproving looks Danny was giving her, and made an effort to join in the conversation. The other two men and their wives were obviously impressed both by Danny and the restaurant. Two out of three wasn't bad averaging, Chris thought cynically, wondering what sort of deal Danny was hoping to arrange with these two very proper Mid-Western Americans and their wives. Danny was a wheeler-dealer in the best sense of the word; he thrived on challenge and crises.

Chris could tell he was still annoyed with her when he took her home. He wanted to come in with her, but she told him firmly in the taxi that he could not. His brief infatuation with her was nearly over, she recognised when he let her get out of the cab, but then what had she expected? It was hardly Danny's fault that she didn't live up to her image. She had grown used to seeing her photograph plastered over the gossip press, generally with that of a casual date, nearly always referred to as her latest 'conquest'. What would those editors say if they knew that in actual fact she was still a virgin?

The thought made her wince. That she was, was only by virtue of the fact that Natalie had interrupted Slater's lovemaking. He had cursed her cousin that day. They had thought themselves alone at his house. He had rung Chris at home just before lunch, and the sound of his voice had sent shivers running down her spine. She had known him a long time. His father had been friendly with her uncle, but he had been away at University and then he had worked in Australia for a couple of years preparing himself for his eventual take-over of his father's farm machinery company. His father had died of a heart attack very unexpectedly and he had come home; tanned, dark-haired, hardened by physical work, Chris had felt an immediate attraction to him.

She had been nineteen, and falling in love with him was the most exhilarating, frightening thing she had ever experienced. She had thought he loved her too. He had told her he did; he had spoken about the future as though it was his intention that they shared it, but in the end it had all meant nothing.

She ought to have guessed that day when Natalie suddenly appeared unexpectedly, but she had simply thought of it as another example of her cousin's bitter jealousy of her.

She had been on holiday from her job in a local travel agents. Slater had rung her at home, suggesting they met for lunch, but when he picked her up, he had told her throatily that the only thing he was hungry for was her. She could remember her excitement even now, she could almost taste the exhilarating fizz of sexual desire and intense adoration. They had gone back to his house—he had inherited it from his father along with the family business; a gracious late Georgian building, not over-large, with a warm, homely atmosphere that Chris loved. She hadn't considered then how wealthy Slater was; she had simply been a girl deeply in love for the first time in her life. If Slater had taken her to the tiniest of terraced houses she would have felt the same.

They hadn't even waited to go upstairs, she remembered painfully. Slater had opened the door to the comfortable living room, and she had been in his arms before it closed behind them, eagerly responding to his kisses, trembling with the desire surging through her body.

They had kissed before, and he had caressed her, but they had never actually made love. Slater knew that she was a virgin. He had asked her, and she had answered him honestly. She had imagined then there had been tenderness as well as anticipation in his eyes but of course, imagination was all it had been. They had been lying on the settee when they were interrupted by Natalie. Chris's blouse had been unfastened, her breasts tender and aroused by Slater's kisses. Natalie had burst in on them completely unexpectedly, half hysterical as she accused Chris of deliberately misleading her about her plans for the day. The only way Chris had been able to calm her down was to go home with her. Slater, she remembered had been tautly angry, and she had thought then it was because he resented her concern for Natalie. Had he even then been making love to her cousin as well? What would have happened if Natalie had not interrupted when she did? What would he have done if he had made both of them pregnant? Hysterical tension bubbled painfully in her throat. Perhaps they could have tossed a coin for him?

The pain grew sharper and she suppressed it from force of habit. Dear God, even now after seven years, the thought of him still made her ache, both emotionally and physically. She had never truly got over him—or more truthfully, she had never truly recovered from the blow of discovering he was not the man she had believed. Not only had she suffered a gruelling sense of rejection, she had also had to endure the knowledge that her judgment was grossly at fault.

She would never forget the day Natalie came to her and told her the truth. It was just a week after she had seen her cousin in Slater's arms.

She had been working all day, and normally Slater picked her up after work. On this occasion though, the girl she worked with told her that Slater's secretary had rung and left a message asking her to go straight round to his house.

She had no car of her own, and it was a two mile walk, but Chris had been too much in love to consider that much of an obstacle. At Slater's house they would be alone. Something he had seemed to avoid since Natalie interrupted them. She knew he was having problems with the company; a matter of securing a very important order which was vital to its continued existence and had put his behaviour down to this.

His car had been parked in the drive when she arrived, and for some reason, which even now she could not really understand, instead of ringing the front door bell she had decided to surprise him by walking in through the sitting room and gave her an uninterrupted view of the settee and its occupants. Her whole body had gone cold as she recognised her cousin's dark head nestled against Slater's shoulder, her arms were round his neck, his head bent over hers. Chris hadn't waited to see any more. On shaky legs she had walked away, dizzy with sickness and pain, unable to come to terms with what she had just witnessed.

She went home and rang Slater from there to

tell him that she wasn't feeling well, hoping against
hope he would mention Natalie's presence; that
there was some explanation for what she had seen,
other than the obvious, but he hadn't.

Natalie had returned many hours later, her
face pale, and her eyes smudged, her whole
bearing one of vindictive triumph and Chris
knew that somehow Natalie knew what she had
witnessed. It was never mentioned by either of
them, at least not then, and Chris had de-
terminedly refused to accept any of Slater's calls
in the week that followed, too hurt to even
confide in her aunt. Later she was glad she had
not done so.

Never in a thousand years would she forget her
shock and pain when Natalie came home and
announced that she was expecting Slater's child.
She had only told Chris at that stage, gloating over
her pain, violently triumphant, almost hysterical
with pleasure. Her cousin had always been
volatile, Chris remembered, always subject to
emotional 'highs' and 'lows'; dangerously so,
perhaps.

She had not got in touch with Slater. The only
thing left for her now was her pride and her
profound thankfulness that she would not share
Natalie's fate; at least she had told herself it was
thankfulness. Even now pain speared her when she
thought of Slater's child, but she dismissed it,
forcing herself to remember the events of that
traumatic day.

Just as soon as she could escape from Natalie
she had gone out, simply walking herself into a
state of numb exhaustion, and that was how Ray
had found her. She hadn't even realised how far

she had walked or that it was getting dark. He had taken her home with him, and although he had questioned her closely, all she would tell him was that she wanted to get away from Little Martin. That was when he had made his suggestion that she should take up modelling as a career. Previously she had only known him casually, but now she found him a warm and helpful friend. When Chris mentioned Natalie's name briefly, not wanting to tell him the truth, Ray had looked angry, and she had gained the impression that he did not like her. That alone had been sufficient to underwrite her trust in him, and it was a trust that had never been misplaced, unlike that she had had for Slater.

She had left that night for London with Ray, and had written to her aunt the next day, explaining that she had worried that her aunt might dissuade her from leaving, giving this as an explanation for her unplanned departure.

A month later Natalie and Slater were married. Her aunt was both stunned and concerned. 'She's so young, Chris,' she had sighed, 'far too young for marriage, but perhaps Slater . . .' she had broken off to frown and say quietly. 'My dear I know that you and Slater . . .'

'We're friends, nothing more,' Chris had quickly assured her, hastily changing the subject, telling her aunt about her new life and making it sound far more exciting than it actually was.

She had worked hard for two years, before suddenly becoming noticed, and was now glad that she had not accepted any of the more dubious assignments that had come her way in those early days. No magazine was ever going to be able to print 'girly' photographs of her simply because none had ever been taken.

She had heard from Natalie once, that was all. A taunting letter, describing in detail her happiness with Slater, and his with her.

'It was very wise of you to leave when you did,' Natalie had written. 'You saved Slater the necessity of telling you he didn't want you any more.'

Chris hadn't bothered replying and she had never heard from either of them since. Now Natalie was dead.

It took her a long time to get to sleep, images from the past haunting her, and then when, at last she did, the impatient jangling of the telephone roused her.

Her room was in darkness, and for a few seconds she was too disorientated to do anything but simply listen to the shrill summons of the 'phone.

At last she made a move to answer it. The crisply precise English accent on the other end of the line surprised her by sounding almost unfamiliar, making her remember how long it was since she had visited her own country. 'I have Mr Smith for you,' the crisp voice announced, the line going dead, before Chris heard the ponderous tones of her aunt's solicitor.

'Chris my dear how are you?'

'Half asleep,' she told him drily. 'Do you realise what time it is here?'

'And do you realise we've been trying to get in touch with you for the last six weeks,' he retaliated. 'I've practically had to subpoena your agent to get this address out of her. Chris, it isn't like you to be so dilatory . . . I'd expected to hear from you before now.'

He must mean about Natalie's death, Chris realised, suddenly coming awake.

'I only got your letter today,' she told him. 'It must have been following me round. What happened? How did Natalie . . .'

'The coroner's verdict was suicide while the balance of her mind was disturbed,' she heard Tom Smith saying, the words reaching her stupefied brain only very slowly. 'I did tell you that in my letter, my dear. Your cousin always was a mite unbalanced, I'm afraid. Your aunt recognised that fact and it used to cause her considerable concern. Roger's mother had a similar temperament.'

Since Tom Smith had known the family for many years Chris did not dispute his comments. Suicide! The word seemed to reverberate painfully inside her skull, resurrecting all her childhood protective instincts towards her cousin. 'Why? Natalie had had everything to live for, a husband, a child . . .'

'It seems that your cousin had been suffering from depression for a long time.' Tom Smith further shocked her by saying. Remorse, hot and sharp, seared through her. Had Natalie needed her, wanted her? Could she have helped her cousin. Pain mingled with guilt; her animosity towards Natalie forgotten, all her bitterness directed towards Slater. Perhaps he had been as unfaithful to Nat as he had her? She should never have blamed her cousin for what had happened; Nat had been an impressionable seventeen, Slater a mature twenty-five. Hatred burned white hot inside her, he had robbed her of everything she thought childishly, all her illusions; her unborn children, and now her only relative. No, not quite her only relative, she realised frowning. There was Nat's little girl . . . Sophie.

'How is Sophie taking it?' she asked Tom Smith automatically, voicing the words almost before she realised she was going to. She had deliberately held herself aloof from all knowledge of Sophie, unable to contemplate the pain of knowing she was Slater's child—the child she had wanted to give him.

'That's why I'm ringing you,' Tom Smith told her, further stunning her. 'She's always been a very withdrawn, introverted child, but now I'm afraid there's cause for serious concern. Sophie hasn't spoken a single word since her mother died.'

Pity for her unknown niece flooded Chris, tears stinging her eyes as she thought of the child's anguish.

'Natalie wouldn't have named you as Sophie's guardian if she hadn't wanted to do so. I know it's asking a lot of you, Chris, but I really think you should come home and see the child.'

Guardian! She was Sophie's guardian? Chris couldn't take it in. Her hand was slippery where it gripped the receiver, all her old doubts and pain coming back, only to be submerged by a wave of pity for Natalie's child.

'But surely Slater . . .' she began huskily, knowing that Slater could never willingly have agreed to Natalie's decision to appoint her as his child's guardian.

'Slater is willing to try anything that might help

Sophie,' Tom Smith astounded her by saying. 'He's desperate, Chris.'

There was a hint of reproach in his voice, and guiltily Chris remembered the unread pages of his letter, which she had discarded. 'Did you write to me about this?' she asked.

'I set everything out in my letter,' he agreed patiently. 'I was very surprised when Natalie came to see me nine months ago and said that she wanted to appoint you as Sophie's guardian, but she was so insistent that I agreed. If only I'd looked more deeply into her reasoning I might have realised how ill she was, but she seemed so calm and reasonable. Her own experience of losing her father had made her aware of how insecure a child could feel with only one parent; if anything should happen to her she wanted to be sure that Sophie would always have someone she could turn to.

'I had no idea then of course, that she hadn't discussed her intentions with Slater, or indeed that you weren't aware of them. There's nothing legally binding on you, of course, and naturally Slater will continue to bring up his daughter, but at the moment he seems unable to reach her. She needs help, Chris, and you might be the only person who can help her.'

'But I'm a stranger to her,' Chris protested, realising fully what Tom was asking of her. How could she return to Little Martin? How could she endure the sight of Slater's child; of Slater himself ... but no, she was over that youthful infatuation. She knew him now for what he was, a weak man too vain to resist the opportunity to seduce a trusting seventeen-year-old.

Had he really loved Natalie or had he simply married her because he had had to? She had had a lucky escape Chris told herself. She could have been Natalie, crushed by marriage to a husband who didn't love her, trapped ... She was letting her imagination run away with her, Chris told herself. She had no reason to suppose that Slater did not love Natalie, perhaps it was even wishful thinking! No! Never!

'Well Chris?'

'I'm coming home.' It wasn't what she had intended to say at all, but now the words were out they could not be retracted.

'Good girl.' Tom Smith's voice approved, and Chris shivered wondering what train of events she had set in motion. She didn't want to go back to Little Martin; she didn't want to see Slater or his child. The past was another country; and one she had sworn she would never re-visit, but it was too late now, she was already committed; committed to a child she had never seen, and remembering instances of Natalie's vindictiveness, she wondered momentarily just why her cousin had named her as her child's guardian. This thought was brushed aside almost instantly by a flood of guilt. If Natalie had been jealous of her, hadn't *she* been jealous too in turn? Hadn't she felt almost ready to kill her cousin when she saw her in Slater's arms. She sighed. All that was over now, Natalie was dead, and in the end, for whatever reason, her cousin had entrusted to her care her child, and she could not in all honour ignore that charge, if only for her aunt's sake.

CHAPTER TWO

LESS than thirty-six hours later when she stepped off a 'plane at Heathrow, Chris still wasn't sure quite how she had got there. A brief call to her agent explaining the situation had resulted in the cancellation of several of her assignments and the postponement of others. It was a testimony to her success that this was allowed to happen, her agent told her drily when she rang from London to tell Chris what she had done.

London was much cooler than New York. To save herself the hassle of a complicated train journey Chris had elected to travel to Little Martin by taxi. The cabbie raised his eyebrows a little when she explained where she wanted to go. The fare, would, she knew, be astronomical, but that was the least of her worries right now. Had she done the right thing? Time alone could answer that. She had acted impulsively, rare for her these days, listening to the voice of her conscience rather than logic. Sophie did not know her and it was almost criminally stupid to imagine the child would respond to her when she could or would not to her own father.

Closing her eyes Chris leaned back into her seat, unaware of her driver's appreciative scrutiny of her through his rear view mirror. Her clothes were simple, but undeniably expensive, and the cabbie wondered what it was that took her to such a remote part of the country in such a rush. She wasn't wearing any rings.

It was three o'clock when the taxi deposited her at Slater's house. She hadn't known where else to go, and since Tom Smith had told her that Slater would be expecting her it had seemed the sensible thing to do. She had only brought one case with her. The local estate agent had the keys to the cottage she had inherited from her aunt and she planned to collect them later on. The cottage would make an ideal base for her whilst she tried to get to know Sophie and decided what to do. It had at one time been let out but the past tenants had left some time ago and now it was empty.

Her ring on the doorbell produced no response and as she waited for someone to appear Chris acknowledged that at least some of the tension infiltrating her body was caused by the thought of meeting Slater.

The house seemed deserted and she rang again, frowning when there was no response. Tom had assured her that Slater would be there. He wanted to see her before she saw Sophie, so Tom had said. Sighing she tried the door handle, half surprised when it turned easily in her hand.

The moment she stepped into the hall memories flooded through her; she had often visited the house with her aunt and uncle who had been friends with Slater's parents, but most of her memories stemmed from those brief months when she had met Slater here, when merely to cycle down the drive and arrive at the house had sent dizzying excitement spiralling through her veins. It had been in this hall that he had first kissed her the afternoon she had come on some now forgotten mission from her aunt. Slater had taken her by surprise, and she had been too stunned to resist. He had seemed half shocked himself, but he had recovered very quickly, making some teasing remark about her being too pretty to resist. That had been the start of it . . .

She sighed, glancing anxiously round the panelled room. Where *was* Slater? She called his name doubtfully, shivering a little in her thin silk dress. What had been warm enough in New York was far from adequate here at home, despite the fact that it was June.

The sitting-room door was half open and drawn by some force greater than her will Chris walked towards it, almost in a trance. It had been here in this room that all her bright, foolish dreams had been destroyed. Like a sleepwalker she walked inside, surprised to find how little had changed. Natalie had loathed the house's traditional decor and she had half expected to find everything different. The sun shone rosily through the french windows, clearly revealing the features of the man stretched out on the settee and Chris came to an abrupt halt, her breathing unexpectedly constricted, almost unbearably conscious of the air burning her skin, as though someone had ripped off an entire layer and left her exposed to unendurable pain. The shock of seeing Slater was a thousand times worse than she had envisaged, and it mattered little that he was oblivious to her presence, apparently fast asleep. Suddenly the intervening years meant nothing, the sophisticated shell of protection she had grown round her during them dissolving and leaving her acutely vulnerable.

His hair was still unmarked by grey, thickly black and ruffled, his frame still as leanly powerful even in sleep. His eyes were closed, lines she didn't remember fanning out from them. His mouth curled downwards, a deep cynicism carved into his skin that she didn't recall, and that shocked her by its unexpectedness. His face was the face of a man who had suffered pain and disillusionment, or so it seemed as she looked at him, and yet where she should have felt glad that this was so, his appearance made her heart ache. Seven years and God alone knew how many thousand miles, they had been apart, and yet as she looked at him Chris found her reaction to him as intense and painful as it had been so long ago.

She couldn't possibly still love him; that was ridiculous, no, what she was experiencing now was something akin to *déjà vu* ... It was only the shock of seeing him so unexpectedly that caused this reaction ... She must remember that he was not and never had been the man she had thought him. She had invested him with qualities, virtues that he had never possessed.

Unaware of what she was doing, she moved closer to him. Tiredness was deeply ingrained in his features. As she moved something clinked against her shoe and she glanced downward to see a half-empty bottle of whisky and a glass. Slater had been drinking? She frowned, and then reminded herself that he was a man whose wife had only recently committed suicide, and that whatever his feelings for Natalie, there must be some feelings of pain and guilt inside him. He moved, frowning in his sleep and the cushion on which he was resting his head slipped on to the floor.

Chris bent automatically to retrieve it, balancing herself against the edge of the settee. Her fingers brushed accidentally against Slater's wrist and he jerked away as though the light contact stung. His shirt was open at the throat, and she could see the dark hair shadowing his skin, thicker now than she remembered, or was it simply that at nineteen she had been less attuned to sheer masculine sexuality than she was now.

Her heart started to thump heavily and she began to draw away, gasping with shock as Slater's fingers suddenly closed round her wrist. His eyes were still closed, a deep frown scoring his forehead. His thumb stroked urgently over the pulse in her wrist, and Chris didn't know what shocked her the most; his caress or her response to it. He was still deeply asleep and she dropped to her knees at his side, gently trying to prise his fingers away without waking him. Anger and tension brought a hectic flush of colour to her skin. Seven years when she had learned to defend herself against every awkward situation there was, and yet here she was reduced to the status of an embarrassed adolescent, simply because a man held her wrist in his sleep.

But Slater wasn't simply *any* man, she acknowledged bitterly and her combined embarrassment and pain sprang not so much from the fact that he was touching her, startling though her reaction to that touch was, as from the knowledge that he undoubtedly believed she was someone else; perhaps Natalie, perhaps not. She couldn't release his fingers. She would have to wake him up. Inwardly fuming, outwardly composed, she leaned over him, trying not to admit her awareness of the

smooth firmness of his flesh beneath his shirt-
sleeve as she touched his arm.

The moment she shook him his eyes flew open.
She had forgotten how mesmeric they could be,
topaz one moment, gold the next. They stared
straight into hers.

'Chrissie . . .' He started to smile, the fingers of
his free hand sliding into her hair and cupping the
back of her head. Too startled to resist, Chris felt
him propel her towards him. Her eyes closed
automatically, her lips parting in anticipation of
his kiss. She might almost never have been away.
His kiss was tender and powerful; she was nineteen
again quivering on the brink of womanhood,
wanting him and yet frightened of that wanting
and his kiss told her that he knew all this and
understood it.

She barely had time to register these facts before
his hold suddenly tightened, his eyes blazing burnt
gold into hers as he withdrew from her. Chris
blinked, slower than he was to make the transition
from past to present, until she saw the biting
contempt in his eyes and recognised that when he
had kissed her he had not been fully awake; not
fully aware of what he was doing.

'So you finally came.' He released her and was
on his feet, whilst she still knelt numbly on the
floor. 'I suppose we ought to be honoured, but I'm
sure you'll forgive us if we don't bring out the
fatted calf. What brought you back, Chrissie?
Guilt? Curiosity?'

Just about to tell him that she had only just
learned of Natalie's death, Chris stumbled to her
feet as she heard sounds outside. The sitting-
room door opened and a smiling plump

woman in her fifties walked in holding the hand of a small child.

Chris breathed in sharply. So this was her niece ... Natalie's child. Slater's child. She couldn't endure to look at him as she studied the little girl, and knew instinctively why Natalie had named her as guardian, just as she knew that her cousin's decision had not been motivated by any of the gentler emotions. Natalie had not changed, she decided helplessly, studying the small face so like her own; the untidy honey-blonde hair, and the general air of dismal hopelessness about the child. By some unkind quirk of fate Sophie could more easily have passed for her daughter than Natalie's, although unlike Chris she had brown eyes.

Chris frowned. Natalie had had blue eyes, and Slater's were amber-gold. No one as far as she knew in either family had possessed that striking combination of blonde hair and velvet-brown eyes, and yet it was familiar to her, so much so that it tugged elusively at her memory.

'There you are, Sophie,' her companion said brightly, 'I told you you were going to have a visitor didn't I?'

The child made no response, not even to the extent of looking at her, Chris realised sadly.

'I have to go and get some shopping now Mr James,' she added to Slater.

'That's fine, Mrs Lancaster. 'You've made up a room for our visitor, I take it?'

'The large guest room,' Mrs Lancaster told Chris with a smile, adding reassuringly to Sophie. 'I'll be back in time for tea, Sophie, and then perhaps tonight your aunt will read your story to you.'

Once again there was no response. Chris ached
to pick the child up and hug her. She looked so
pitifully vulnerable, so lost, and hurt somehow,
and yet she sensed that it would be best not to
approach her. She frowned as she remembered
what Slater had said about a room for her. She
must tell him that she would be staying at the
cottage. She glanced at her watch, remembering
that she still had to collect the keys.

'Bored with us already?' Slater drawled sardonically.

Chris saw Sophie conceal a betraying wince at
her father's tone and she frowned, wondering what
had caused the child's reaction. Had Slater
perhaps often spoken to Natàlie in that sarcastic
voice? Children saw and felt more than their
parents gave them credit for, but she could hardly
question Slater on his relationship with her cousin.
Did he know why Natalie had appointed her as
Sophie's co-guardian?

She glanced at him bitterly. Perhaps he had
shared Natalie's resentment that their child should
so much favour her. She shuddered to think of the
small unkindnesses Sophie could have suffered at
Natalie's hands; torments remembered from her
own childhood, and then reminded herself that
Sophie was Natalie's child, and that as usual she
was letting her imagination run away with her.

Chris looked up to find Sophie studying her
warily, as she crept closer to her father. His hand
reached out to enfold her smaller one, the smile he
gave her was reassuring. A huge lump closed off
Chris's throat. She had been wrong about one
thing at last. Patently Slater did love his small
daughter—very much. There was pain as well as

love in the gold eyes as they studied the small pale face.

'I can't think why Natalie specified that I was to be her guardian,' Chris murmured unguardedly.

Almost at once Slater's expression hardened. 'Can't you?' he said curtly. Sophie tensed, and as though he sensed her distress, he stopped speaking, smiling warmly at the child before continuing, 'I'd better show you to your room.'

'That won't be necessary.' Chris was cool and very much in control now. She gave him the same cold brief smile she reserved for too-eager males. It normally had an extremely dampening effect, but Slater seemed quite unimpressed. 'I'll be staying at the cottage,' she continued. 'In fact I'd better get round to Reads and collect the keys. They've been keeping the place aired and cleaned for me.'

'Chris!' There was anger and bitterness reverberating in his voice, and Chris saw Sophie tauten again. Slater must have been aware of her tension too, because he broke off to say soothingly, 'It's all right Sophie, I'm not cross. We have to talk,' he told Chris levelly, 'and it would be much easier to do so if you stayed here, but I remember enough about you to realise that you'll go your own way now, just as you did in the past. I'll walk out to your car with you.'

No doubt so that he could say the things to her he wanted to without upsetting Sophie. It was strange, Chris reflected painfully. All these years she had deliberately refused to think about Slater's child, and yet now that she had seen her, she felt none of the resentment or pain she had expected. Sophie was simply a very unhappy, vulnerable child whom she ached to comfort and help, but she was sensible enough to know that the first approach would have to come from Sophie herself.

'I don't have a car,' she told Slater coolly. 'If I can leave my case here for an hour I'll come back and collect it once I've got the keys for the cottage. I can use my aunt's Mini to drive back in.'

Slater's smile was derisive. 'Please yourself Chris,' he drawled mockingly. 'I'd offer to take you, but I can't leave Sophie, and she isn't too keen on riding in the car.'

Chris frowned, but Sophie's face bore out her father's statement, she looked tense and frightened.

It took her longer than she had anticipated to walk to the village—she had forgotten that she was no longer a teenager and accustomed to the almost daily walk. The estate agent expressed concern when she told him her intentions.

'But my dear Chris, the place has been empty for nearly two years . . .'

'I arranged for it to be kept cleaned and aired,' Chris reminded him frowningly.

'Which we have done, but the roof developed a leak during the winter, it needs completely re-thatching. I have written to tell you,' he told her half apologetically, and Chris sighed, hearing the faintly accusatory note in his voice. 'Using your aunt's Mini is completely out of the question. I doubt you could even get it started. I've got a better idea. My sister has a small car which I know she won't mind you borrowing. She's in Greece at the moment on holiday, and won't be back for several weeks. How long are you intending to stay in Little Martin?'

'I'm not sure yet,' Chris told him, accepting his offer of the loan of a car, but refusing to allow him to book a room at the village inn for her. However bad the cottage was, she could stay there one night, surely? She was already befuddled with all the decisions she had had to make recently. Tomorrow she could decide where she was going to stay. It would have to be somewhere close to Sophie otherwise there would be no point in her visit.

After she had collected Susan Bagshaw's small Ford and thanked Harold Davies for the loan of it, Chris drove straight back to Slater's house. She had been longer than she expected and her heart thumped anxiously as she approached the house. Unbidden the memory of Slater's warmly persuasive kiss made her mouth soften and her pulses race.

Stop it, she warned herself angrily. He had kissed her almost as a reflex action, his true feelings towards her more than clearly revealed in his attitude to her once he was properly awake. What was the matter with her anyway? She had been kissed by dozens of men since she left Little Martin. But their touch had never affected her as Slater's had done, she admitted tiredly. Perhaps now that she was back in Little Martin, it was time for her to face up to the fact that she had never really overcome Slater's rejection of her; that her feelings for him had never properly died; principally because she had never allowed herself a true mourning period. She had rushed straight from the discovery of his infidelity into the hectic world of modelling, refusing to even allow herself to think about what had happened. Had she really come back simply for Sophie's sake, or had some instinct, deeper and more powerful than logic drawn her back, forcing her to face the past and to come to terms with it, because until she did, she would never really be free to love another man?

She could admit that now, just as she could admit how barren and empty her life was. All the things she had really wanted from life had been torn from her and so she had been forced to set herself alternative goals, but career success had never really attracted her; the values instilled in her by her aunt still held good. At heart she was still that same nineteen-year-old. She wanted a husband and children, Chris admitted, surprised to discover how deep this need was, but Slater stood firmly in the way of her ever forming a permanent relationship with any other man; as did her life-style. The men she met were not marriage material. Disturbed by the ghosts she had let loose inside herself, Chris parked the car and walked towards the front door.

It was several minutes after she had rung the bell when Slater appeared. He had changed his clothes and in the checked shirt and jeans he could almost have been the Slater of seven years ago. Chris felt her muscles tense as he invited her in. As he stepped back her body brushed briefly against his in the close confines of the half-opened door. Her nerve endings reacted wildly, shivering spasms of awareness flickering over her skin, whilst she schooled her face to betray nothing.

'What happened to the Mini?' he asked once she was inside.

'Harold didn't think it would start. He's loaned me his sister's car in the interim.'

'What did you do? Flash those sea-green eyes at him? You'll have to be careful, Chris, this isn't New York. Husband-stealing isn't acceptable practice down here.'

Anger burned chokingly inside her. Who was he to dare to criticise what he assumed to be her way of life? After what he had done to her, how dare he ... She bit back the angry retort trembling on the tip of her tongue. Tom Smith had warned her that should he wish, Slater could protest against and possibly overrule Natalie's will. If she wanted to fulfil the role Natalie had cast for her she must try to maintain some semblance of normality between Slater and herself.

'Where's Sophie?' she asked hesitantly, trying to fill the bitter silence stretching between them.

'In bed,' Slater told her, adding sardonically, 'Children often are at this time of night. It's gone eight, and she's had a particularly tiring day. Meeting strangers always seems to have a bad effect on her.'

He had no need to remind her of her status, Chris thought tiredly. No one was more aware of it than she; it made her feel very guilty. There was something about Sophie that touched her almost painfully. Perhaps it was the physical resemblance to herself; the memories of the pain and loneliness of her own childhood, once her parents had died and before she realised the depth of the bond that could exist between her aunt and herself.

'I don't know exactly why you've come here Chris,' he added tautly, 'but Sophie isn't a toy to be picked up, played with for a while, and then put down when you're bored. She's a very vulnerable, unhappy little girl.'

'She's also my only living relative,' Chris said unsteadily, 'and I feel I owe it to Natalie to do whatever I can for her.'

'Is that how you see her?' he jeered unkindly. 'As a responsibility? She's a responsibility it's taken you damn near six weeks to acknowledge, Chris. Sophie doesn't need that sort of half-hearted, guilt-induced interest.'

'I've only just received Tom Smith's letter,' Chris protested angrily.

'Why? Or is it that you only return to your own address at six weekly intervals, just to check that it's still there?'

His inference was plain and dark colour scorched Chris's face. Let him think what he wished, she thought bitterly. Let him imagine she had a score of lovers if that was what he wanted. Why not? It was far better than him knowing the truth. That there hadn't been a single lover, because in her heart she was still aching for his lovemaking . . . still grieving for what she had lost.

'I didn't want you here,' she heard him saying curtly to her, 'but Natalie did appoint you as Sophie's joint guardian, although I think we both know that can't have sprung from any altruistic impulse.'

Hard eyes impaled her as she swung a startled face towards him. But then why should she be so surprised? Naturally Natalie would have told him how much she hated her. After all in the early days at least they had been deeply in love; in love enough for him to have discarded her in the cruellest and most painful way he could. 'I suppose Natalie did resent the fact that she looks like me,' Chris agreed bleakly.

Slater's face was grim. 'In the circumstances it hardly endeared the child to her,' he agreed, and Chris frowned a little. At times he had a manner of speaking about Sophie that seemed to distance her from him, almost as though the little girl were not his daughter, and yet there was such an obvious bond of affection between them. Before she could question him further about his remark he went on to say, 'Tom Smith seems to think you might be able to reach Sophie, and so does John Killigrew, the doctor in charge of her case at the hospital. Sarah and I aren't so sure.'

Sarah? Chris's heart pounded. Was this the explanation for Natalie's suicide. Did Slater have another woman?

'Sarah?' she questioned lightly, avoiding his eyes, in case he read in them what she was thinking. Much as she had cause to resent her cousin, she could only feel sympathy with her, if she too had suffered the pain of being rejected by Slater. At least in her case all he had destroyed was her ability to love and trust, while in Natalie's . . .

'Sarah is the psychotherapist in charge of Sophie's case. Such behaviour isn't entirely unknown in children and generally springs from a deep-seated trauma. Until we discover what that trauma is it is unlikely that she will speak, although there are various ways in which we can encourage her, but if you do intend to stay and help, Sarah will brief you on these herself.

Chris stared at him nonplussed. 'I thought the trauma was obvious,' she said unsteadily. 'Sophie has lost her mother in the most distressing way . . . Surely that . . .'

'Sarah doesn't believe that is the cause and neither do I.' He was almost brusque, turning slightly away from her so that his face was in the shadows. 'Sophie and Natalie did not get on. Natalie spent very little time with the child.'

Chris was not entirely convinced.

'Why did Nat commit suicide?' she asked him abruptly.

He swung round, the shadows etching the bones forming his face, stealing from it every trace of colour. His eyes glittered febrilely over her as he studied her, his body tense with an emotion she could not define.

'Tom Smith has already told you. She was mentally disturbed.'

'You don't seem particularly concerned.' It was a dangerous thing to say, and she almost wished it unsaid when he continued to stare at her.

'What is it you want me to say Chris?' he demanded bitterly at last. 'Natalie and I elected to go our separate ways a long, long time ago. My main concern now is Sophie. She's already suffered enough at the hands of your cousin. I don't intend to let you increase that suffering. Just remember that while you're here I'll be watching every step you take. Do anything that affects Sophie adversely and you'll be leaving.'

'I'm not leaving Little Martin until I see Sophie running about, laughing and chattering as a six-year-old should,' Chris retaliated fiercely, the commitment she had just made half shocked her, almost as though she had been impelled to take the first step down a road she hadn't intended to traverse. Slater was still watching her and fantastically, despite his cold eyes and grim mouth she had the impression that he was pleased by her reaction, although she could not have said why. Imagination, she told herself sardonically. Slater could have no reason at all for wanting her to stay.

'That's quite a commitment you just made,' he told her softly. 'Are you capable of seeing it through I wonder?'

She bent to pick up her case, pushing the honey blonde cloud of hair obscuring her vision out of the way, impatiently, as she stood up to face him.

'Just watch me,' she told him grimly.

She was outside and in the car before she realised that she had not made any arrangements for the following day. A quick mental check informed her that it would be Friday—how travelling distorted one's sense of time—that meant that Slater would be working. She would call on him early in the morning and tackle him about what access she could have to Sophie. Feeling as though she had cleared at least one obstacle, she put the car in gear and set out for the cottage.

CHAPTER THREE

THE lane which led to the cottage and which she remembered as scenic and rural, was dark, almost oppressively so, the lane itself badly rutted in places, and Chris heaved a small sigh of relief when at last she picked out the familiar low crouching outline of the cottage in the car's headlights.

Parking outside she hurried up the uneven paved path. The lock was faintly rusty and she broke a nail as she applied leverage to the key. Grimacing ruefully she stepped inside, flicking on the light automatically. Her eyes widened in shock as she stared round the sitting room. Damp stains mildewed one of the walls; the cottage felt cold, and even worse, smelled faintly musty. She remembered now that her aunt had always insisted on a small fire even in summer, and that she had often expressed concern about the building's damp course too. As a teenager she had paid scant attention to these comments, but now she was forced to acknowledge their veracity.

Why had no one written to her; told her how much the cottage was deteriorating? Or perhaps they had and their letters were still following her round the world. Sighing Chris made her way through the living room and into the kitchen. Here too signs of decay and neglect were obvious. The cottage was clean enough but desolate somehow, and so cold and damp that the atmosphere struck right through to her bones. The dining room was no better, more patches of damp marring the plaster. With a heavy heart Chris made her way upstairs. The roof needed re-thatching John had told her, and during the winter it had leaked. He had added that they had made what temporary repairs they could, but all her worse fears were confirmed when she opened the first bedroom door and walked inside. She and Natalie had once shared this room; its contours, every crack in its walls were unbearably familiar to her, as was the faint, but unmistakable perfume that also lingered in the air. Natalie's perfume, heavy and oriental, at seventeen she was far too young to wear such a sophisticated fragrance, but she had insisted on doing so nonetheless, and its scent still hung on the air. Surely after six years it ought to have died, Chris thought frowningly. Unless of course Natalie had been here more recently. But why? She had flatly refused to take on any responsibility for the cottage when Natalie had been forced to have her aunt moved away from it. It could moulder away to dust was what Tom Smith told her she had said when she asked him to get in touch with her. She touched the cover of one of the single beds absently, withdrawing her fingers as they met the damp fabric. She shivered suddenly, noticing the mildew clinging to the cover. This had been her bed ... She smiled wryly to herself. She had chosen the quilt herself. Natalie had chosen exactly the same thing, and then had burned a hole in her own with a cigarette while smoking secretly in bed. Absently her fingers smoothed the fabric, tensing as they found the small betraying burn mark. This was Natalie's quilt. What was it doing on her bed?

Memories of Natalie's possessiveness during their shared childhood flooded her. Natalie had hated her even touching anything of hers. She would never have allowed her quilt to be placed on Chris's bed. That was all in the past, Chris reminded herself. No doubt whoever cleaned the cottage had mixed up the quilts. She turned round and walked out of the room, shutting away the memories and the lingering traces of Natalie's perfume. She couldn't possibly sleep in that room, it was far too damp.

Her aunt's bedroom showed the same distressing signs of neglect. Now she knew why Slater had offered her a bedroom she thought wryly. She would have to stay here tonight. She could hardly go back now and wake up the whole household. So where did that leave her? If she wanted to get close to Sophie she would either have to take a room at the pub or . . . or swallow her pride and ask Slater if his offer of a room was still open. Much as she wanted to help Sophie she didn't know if she could cope with sharing the same house as Slater.

She wasn't nineteen any more she reminded herself wryly. What was she afraid of? That Slater would try to take up where they had left off? Hardly likely. No, tomorrow she would just have to go cap in hand to him and ask for his help, much as she resented the idea. But that was tomorrow. She still had to cope with tonight. Sleeping in either of the bedrooms was out which left only the living room. Shivering slightly at the thought she remembered that her aunt used to

keep spare bedding in the airing cupboard. If it
was still there, perhaps it might at least be dry.
While she was here she would have to get a builder
in to check over the cottage and put it to rights;
put in a new damp course and renew the roof.
Until that was done no one could possibly live
here.

As she walked towards the bathroom, she
glanced automatically at the small chest in the
landing alcove and then frowned. Two cigarette
butts lay in the ashtray. The hairs on the back of
her neck prickled warningly and she suppressed
the desire to turn round and look behind her.
Obviously they had been left there by the cleaner.
And yet as she entered the bathroom Chris had the
distinct impression that something was not quite
right . . . Pushing aside the notion as fanciful she
opened the airing cupboard, relieved to discover a
pile of bedding there that felt dry to the touch. The
house had an immersion heater so at least she
would be able to have a warm bath before curling
up downstairs on one of the chairs, although she
didn't anticipate getting a good deal of sleep.
Coming back had resurrected far more memories
than she had anticipated, or was it Slater's briefly
tender kiss that had stirred up all the tension she
could feel inside herself? Why had Natalie
committed suicide? Would they ever know?
Mentally disturbed was how Slater had described
her and whilst it was true that she had always had a
tendency towards hysteria, especially when she
couldn't get her own way, she had always thirsted
for life with a tenacity that Chris simply could not
envisage disappearing overnight.

She woke up as she had expected to, cold and

stiff, shivering in the early morning light. It was seven o'clock. In the past Slater had always left for the factory at eight thirty, which didn't leave her much time to see him.

Bathing and dressing in fresh clothes, she brushed her hair, leaving her skin free of make-up. Her stomach growled protestingly, reminding her how long it was since she had had something to eat, as she hurried out to the car.

She drove up towards Slater's house slowly, dreading the moment when she must face him. Mrs Lancaster opened the door to her, her kind face creased in concern as she saw Chris's pale set face.

'Is Slater in?' Chris asked tensely.

'He's just having his breakfast,' she told her. 'You can go straight through. I'll go and get another cup, you look as though you could do with something to drink.'

Chris knocked hesitantly on the door and then opened it. Dressed in a formal business suit, Slater looked far more formidable than he had done the previous day. He was drinking a cup of coffee, the cup raised to his lips, his eyebrows drawing together as he saw her. He replaced the cup and folded the newspaper he had been studying.

'Good morning. I trust you slept well.' His voice was coolly derisive and Chris had to stop herself from flushing, knowing that he must know exactly how uncomfortable a night she had had.

'Not very,' she managed to respond. 'I hadn't realised the cottage had become so dilapidated. My own fault I suppose . . .' She saw Slater flick back a cuff to glance at his watch, the gold band glistening among the dark hairs, and she had to fight down a sense of hostility that he should make it so plain that he was anxious to be free of her company.

'Let's cut the small talk shall we?' he said curtly. 'I'm sure you haven't come here at this time of the morning to discuss the work that needs to be done on the cottage. What do you want?'

God how she hated him, Chris seethed, loathing the way he was reducing her to the role of begging.

He must know why she was here; he had to, and yet he was doing everything he could to make it hard for her.

The arrival of his housekeeper with a cup and a fresh pot of coffee provided a welcome break, but as soon as she had gone, his eyes hardened to icy coldness, and he made no move to offer her a drink, Chris noticed, her resentment increasing by the second. If it wasn't for Sophie she would turn on her heel and walk out of here right now.

'Well Chris?' The curt impatience of his voice lacerated her tender nerves.

Her voice husky with anger she said tensely, 'I came to ask if your offer of a room was still open. Obviously I can't stay at the cottage . . .'

The smile he gave her wasn't encouraging. It made her heart miss a beat and then start to thud unevenly. 'Well now, I seem to remember yesterday that you were most vehement in refusing to stay here. Quite a change of heart.'

'Yesterday I thought I would be able to stay at the cottage.' Chris replied as evenly as she could, hating the way he was making her explain what he already knew—and had known yesterday. All the time she had been refusing to stay here he had known the state of the cottage and that she would have to retract. Fury brought a dark flush of colour to her skin as she continued bitterly, 'Unlike you I didn't realise the state it was in . . .'

'What are you trying to do Chris,' he interrupted sardonically. 'Blame me for your own rash impulsiveness? That was ever your way wasn't it—to blame others for your own failings?'

The injustuce of his comment and the bitter way in which he voiced it took her breath away. Tears stung her eyes, much to her chagrin. That was it. She couldn't take any more. Turning her back on him she was just about to walk out when he said quietly, 'The offer *is* still open, and now if you'll excuse me, it's time I was leaving. Sarah will be arriving just after ten. Mondays, Wednesdays and Fridays, she spends two hours a morning with Sophie. And now if you'll excuse me.'

He was standing up and opening the door before Chris could speak. She wanted to fling his offer in his face, to tell him that she didn't need his room, but she forced herself to hold her tongue. Surely she had learned in the last six years to control her temper? Puzzled she glanced at the closed door. In fact she couldn't remember a single instance when she had lost it, and yet here she was dangerously close to boiling point after the exchange of barely a dozen words with Slater.

Before she could dwell too deeply on her thoughts Mrs Lancaster came in, smiling again. 'I'll just get you some breakfast,' she offered, 'and then I'll take you up to see your room and Sophie.'

Gratefully Chris sat down. At least Mrs Lancaster appeared not to resent her presence. When the older woman came back with grapefruit and toast, Chris asked her to stay. 'It would help me to know something of Sophie's routine,' she told her. 'I know so little about her.'

'Poor little mite, it's a shame,' Mrs Lancaster murmured. 'Bright little thing she was too at one time. Worships her father she does . . .'

'And her mother?' Chris questioned. 'Did Sophie get on well with her mother?'

'I couldn't say.' The housekeeper avoided her eyes. 'Always in and out was Mrs James. Always here, there and everywhere.'

In other words Natalie had tended to neglect her child, Chris thought reading between the lines, but how did Sophie's inability to speak tie in with that? Perhaps Sarah would be able to tell her more; perhaps it wouldn't be a bad idea to see if she could find something to read on the subject.

While she ate her breakfast Mrs Lancaster outlined Sophie's routine. 'I normally get her up about nine; she has breakfast, and then if Sarah isn't coming she goes out to play in the garden.

'In the afternoon if it's fine I take her out for a walk. Mr James normally plays with her for a couple of hours when he comes in—devoted to her he is, and so patient.'

'She's almost six,' Chris murmured. 'What about school?'

'Doing quite well at playschool she was until this happened. She still reads a lot and Mr James gets special books for her; you know, so that he can teach her himself, but they won't accept her at the village school the way she is just now.'

Poor Sophie, Chris's heart went out to her. Already she was an outcast—different from her peers; if only she could help her in some way.

Tentatively she asked Mrs Lancaster if it would
be possible for her and Sophie to have breakfast
with Slater, and to her relief the housekeeper
agreed. 'More company is what she needs,' she
told her, 'a proper family atmosphere if you know
what I mean. I always thought . . .' She broke off
and looked slightly flustered, and diplomatically
Chris didn't probe. The housekeeper must know
more about Slater and Natalie's life together than
anyone else, and perhaps in time she might be able
to learn something from her that would give her a
clue as to why Natalie should take her own life.

Finishing her breakfast, she asked if she could
accompany the housekeeper upstairs when she
went to wake Sophie.

The little girl was awake when they walked into
her room—a dream of a little girl's room,
decorated in sugar candy pinks and frills.

'Chose all the decorations in here himself Mr
James did,' Mrs Lancaster told Chris proudly
watching her survey the room. 'All new it is . . .'

'Oh . . . what was it like before?' Chris
questioned wondering if it had been a good idea to
take away things that were familiar no matter how
well-intentioned the action had been.

Mrs Lancaster's lips compressed. She frowned
slightly as she looked at Sophie, and then said at
last. 'Mrs James always said there wasn't much
point in doing a room up specially for her, claimed
the child wouldn't appreciate it. Downright cruel
she was to her sometimes,' she added, lowering her
voice.

Biting her lip Chris glanced across at the bed.
Sophie was lying there watching them, and sudden
memory of her own childhood came to her.

Without pausing to think Chris went across to her and sat down, picking up a framed photograph off the chest by the bed. In it Sophie was smiling up at her father. Natalie was not included in the print. 'What a lovely photograph of Sophie this is,' Chris exclaimed, holding the frame out to Mrs Lancaster. 'She looks so pretty when she smiles.' It was no less than the truth, but Chris had had a vivid memory of Natalie at six saying furiously that she would not share her bedroom with Chris and that she hated, hated her plain ugly cousin.

Chris had been heartbroken at her rejection, and for years had genuinely thought that she was ugly; a view that Natalie had been at pains to reinforce. Could she have done the same thing to Sophie? It seemed impossible, but the human brain was a strange thing. Natalie would have bitterly resented having a child who looked so much like her, Chris knew and perhaps there had been occasions when she had taken out her hatred of her cousin on her child.

The pansy brown eyes flickered from Chris to the photograph, but the small face remained solemn and stiff. Where had she seen that combination of fair hair and brown eyes before Chris wondered idly. It was so familiar she felt she ought to be able to remember and yet she could not.

'What a pretty pink dress too,' Chris exclaimed, refusing to give up. 'I used to have a dress like that when I was a little girl. Is pink your favourite colour Sophie?' she asked the little girl, addressing her directly for the first time.

Sophie's only response was to look behind Chris at the housekeeper.

'Mrs James used to dress her in dungarees most of the time,' she told Chris. 'Said there wasn't much point in dressing her up, although she spent enough on her own clothes.' She sniffed disapprovingly and then said to Sophie. 'Come on now young lady. Time you were getting up.'

Not wanting to overwhelm Sophie Chris got to her feet. 'I'll meet you both downstairs, shall I?' she suggested, smiling at Sophie, leaving her with the other woman.

Exactly on the dot of ten a small estate car stopped outside the house. The girl who got out was slim, with chestnut hair and a very self-possessed expression. Chris disliked her on sight, and wondered at her atavistic response. It wasn't like her to take an instant dislike to anyone.

Nevertheless she introduced herself pleasantly while Mrs Lancaster went to get Sophie and make them some coffee, trying to make conversation.

'Slater tells me you come here three mornings a week? How is Sophie responding so far?'

'It's too early to say yet,' the other girl said dismissively.

Was Sarah slightly defensive? Chris could not tell, but she knew that her dislike was reciprocated when Sarah added curtly, 'You know that neither Slater or I want you here? You can't do anything to help Sophie. She needs expert care and attention.'

'Her mother appointed me as her co-guardian,' Chris interrupted quietly, determined to keep her temper and not allow herself to be rattled by the way Sarah banded Slater and herself together, and firmly placed Chris as their enemy.

'Her mother!' Sarah smiled with derision.

'Natalie never gave a damn about the child . . . she hated her from the moment she was born. If she ever thought of Sophie at all it was simply as a pawn she could use against Slater.'

'You seem to know an awful lot about my cousin and her husband.' Chris spoke before she could stop herself, hating the triumphant gleam shining in Sarah's too pale blue eyes as she returned, 'Slater and I are old friends . . .'

Old friends and new lovers? Chris wondered, stunned by the spearing pain jolting through her body.

When Mrs Lancaster returned with Sophie, she was glad of the excuse to escape.

'I'll take you up to your room now,' the housekeeper offered. 'It does have its own bathroom.'

On the landing she walked past Sophie's room and two other doors, hesitating for a second outside one before passing on to a third, and opening the door into a pleasantly decorated guest room. Chris's case was already on the bed; the room had attractive views over the gardens, the adjoining bathroom decorated in a similar style to the bedroom.

How long would she be staying here she wondered? How long could she *endure* to stay here? An unpleasant thought struck her. If Sarah and Slater were lovers, did she stay here?

Why should it concern her, she asked herself hardily. She had no romantic interest in Slater now. That was all dead. But was it?

More to distract her thoughts than anything else she asked Mrs Lancaster briefly, 'Slater and Natalie . . . which room . . .'

'Mrs James had her own room,' Mrs Lancaster told her non-committally—'the door next to this . . .' She fidgeted for a moment and then added anxiously. 'All her things are still in there, I was wondering if you could possibly sort through them . . .'

'But surely Slater . . .' Chris protested, still trying to come to terms with the fact that Slater and Natalie had apparently had separate rooms. At whose instigation? Mrs Lancaster had already intimated that Natalie spent a good deal of time away from the house, but how long had Slater and Sarah . . .

'Mr James just told me to get rid of everything and close up the room, but I felt I couldn't. Some of her clothes were very expensive . . .'

Chris could understand Mrs Lancaster's dilemma. 'Of course I'll go through them,' she agreed, thinking that distasteful though the task promised to be, it was something she owed her cousin.

Chris did not see Sarah go. Mrs Lancaster came out into the garden to tell her that lunch was ready and explained that the other woman had left.

Sophie was very subdued over lunch, keeping her eyes fixed on her plate. What had happened that was so traumatic that it had stopped her from talking? And not just from talking, Chris acknowledged, covertly watching her. Sophie was a very withdrawn little girl, flinching away from almost every physical contact, locked up inside herself.

After lunch Mrs Lancaster explained that she was going shopping. Sophie normally went with her but when Chris suggested that the little girl might want to stay behind with her, she was both surprised and pleased to see the fair head nod.

'She's taken to you,' Mrs Lancaster told Chris when Sophie went upstairs to clean her teeth. 'Apart from those brown eyes she's the spitting image of you too.'

'Umm, genes are a funny thing,' Chris agreed. She had spotted a pile of children's books in the sitting room. The afternoon was sunny and warm, and after choosing a book for herself from Slater's well-stocked bookshelves she headed back to the dining room, where as she expected, Sophie was waiting. Just because the little girl refused to speak it didn't mean she did not hear—and understand, Chris reminded herself. She couldn't force Sophie to accept her, to give her her confidence, but ... Coming to a decision she began speaking, talking quietly, addressing her comments to herself.

'It's such a lovely afternoon I think I'll go out into the garden. If I can find a deckchair somewhere I could sit down and read. Perhaps I'll find one in the garage.'

Without looking to see Sophie's reaction she headed for the kitchen and the back door, pleased to see that the little girl was following her. The drab, oversize dungarees she was wearing did nothing for her thin, tense little body, and Chris made a mental note to go out and buy her some new clothes. Perhaps she might even be able to take Sophie with her.

As she had expected she found some garden chairs in the garage, picking one up, she strolled round to the large back lawn, Sophie at her heels.

All the time she was walking she kept on talking—about the house and the village—about the changes she had found—about her aunt and her own childhood, but never mentioning Sophie's mother.

When she finally sat down and opened her book Sophie was still beside her.

'Umm this looks a good story.' She flicked a glance at the silent child as she opened one of Sophie's books and started to read aloud from it.

Sophie was standing six feet away watching her. Chris read slowly and patiently, occasionally lifting her eyes from the page to remark on her surroundings. Sophie gave no signs of responding, but she was still there, watching her motionlessly.

Chris was more than halfway through the book before she felt Sophie move. Her heart leapt tensely. Had she got bored and walked away or ... She dare not lift her eyes from the printed page, and was only able to expel her breath properly when the child's shadow fell across her lap as Sophie crept nearer. She was still standing beside her chair when Chris came to the end of the story.

At least she had established contact with Sophie if nothing else, she thought elatedly. The little girl had not rejected her as she had feared. What had Natalie told Sophie about her if anything? Had she drawn comparisons between them? Sighing frustratedly Chris picked up another of Sophie's books. There was so much that was a puzzle to her and it was one she had no way of solving without Sophie's co-operation. She had reached automatically for the next book in the pile, and was startled when Sophie's brown fingers pushed her hand away, and then extracted another book thrusting it towards her.

The book was old and tattered, and suddenly unbearably familiar. It was one of her own Chris recognised. A book she had received from her parents on her last birthday before they died. Carefully smoothing over the battered cover she remembered how precious the book had once been to her—a symbol of all that she had lost. She had left it behind at the cottage when she left along with all her other treasures. But where had Sophie got it from?

Frowning slightly, she suddenly realised that the little girl was watching her, her eyes imploring. With an unexpected movement she opened the book as it lay on Chris's lap, pointing to where Chris had long ago inscribed her name.

Sophie knew! Somehow the little girl had divined what had been in her mind and this was her way of showing her that she did know who she was. Emotion overwhelmed her, and reacting without thinking Chris did what she had promised herself she would not do, reaching out to hug the tense wiry body braced against her. Too late she remembered that she had told herself she would let Sophie be the one to do the approaching. 'Oh Sophie . . .' She released her shakily, brushing the fair hair out of the brown eyes. 'Yes that was once my book,' she told her, trying to sound calm. 'My parents gave it to me when I was a little girl— before I went to live with your mummy, but where did you get it?'

Instantly Sophie tensed, her brown eyes frightened and wary. Dear God, Sophie thought she was going to be cross with her. 'No no, darling,' she said softly, 'I'm not cross. I'm glad you found it. Do you want me to read to you from it?'

The fear retreated and Sophie nodded her head guardedly, leaning against the side of Chris's chair as she started to read. The warmth of her slight body was a reminder to Chris of all she herself had never had.

Slater's child, Chris thought painfully glancing at her downbent head, and yet she could see nothing of Slater in her. Because perhaps she didn't want to?

She stopped reading and looked at Sophie, remarking softly, 'You know I think you would be much more comfortable sitting on my knee. What do you think? Would you like that?'

She held her breath, half expecting rejection. She was amazed that Sophie had responded to her as well as she had, but when the fair head nodded she managed to conceal her elation and say very calmly. 'Come on then, let me lift you up.'

She was still sitting there an hour later when Mrs Lancaster returned, the older woman's eyebrows lifting when she came into the garden and saw them.

'She's asleep,' Chris told her smiling at her.

'My goodness, you're honoured, but then I could tell she'd taken to you right from the start. Never left you, her eyes didn't yesterday.'

'I can't help wondering what Natalie told her about me,' Chris felt drawn to confide in the other woman. 'She and I never got on. She used to say I was ugly . . .'

'Aye, she had a nasty way with words when she wanted,' Mrs Lancaster agreed. 'Many's the time I found the kiddie crying after she'd had a go at her.'

'Slater doesn't seem to think that Sophie's

trauma is as a result of her mother's death. He seems to think there's something else.'

'I must admit I didn't expect her to take it so hard. After all she didn't see that much of her, but then you never know with kiddies.'

Not wanting to seem too curious about her cousin's private affairs Chris did not ask any more questions, letting the housekeeper continue indoors.

Tomorrow she would make a start on Natalie's room, she decided as she carried Sophie inside a little later on.

She heard the 'phone ring as she walked inside, and then it stopped as Mrs Lancaster answered it.

'That was Mr James,' she told Chris ten minutes later. 'Said he wouldn't be in to dinner tonight and that you were to eat without him.'

'Did he say when he would be back?' Did her voice tremble betrayingly Chris wondered, hating herself for asking the question. What business of hers were Slater's comings and goings?

'No, he didn't.'

So Slater wouldn't be eating with them tonight. Why should that make her feel so restless and tense. Was he taking Sarah out to dinner perhaps. White-hot shafts of pain burned through her flesh. What was the matter with her, Chris asked herself. Surely she wasn't jealous?

CHAPTER FOUR

CHRIS woke abruptly from a deep sleep, completely disorientated and not knowing why she had woken until she heard the thin keening sound again. It shivered through her, raising goosebumps of flesh on her body, compelling an automatic reaction that had her on her feet and hurrying towards her bedroom door.

The sound was one of an animal in pain and terror—or a small child and Chris headed instinctively for Sophie's room, not bothering to switch on lights in her haste to reach the little girl.

A nightmare scene greeted her. Sophie's curtains were open, moonlight picking out the rigid figure of the little girl as she sat bolt upright in her bed; her eyes wide and staring, a tormented almost unearthly sound issuing from her throat, making Chris shudder in sympathetic response.

As she reached the bed, Slater's authoritative voice said curtly from behind her, 'Leave her . . . don't touch her. I'll handle this.'

He pushed past her, and sat down on the bed, taking Sophie in his arms, murmuring soft words of comfort to her, until the rigidity left her body. Chris expelled her own breath in reaction, not realising how tense she had been until she did so. Very gently Slater laid the sleeping child back on the mattress, watching her broodingly for several seconds before drawing the covers up over her. Sophie's eyes were closed now, her body relaxed and at peace. For the first time Chris became aware of the thinness of her own muslin nightdress. She had responded automatically to Sophie's distress, not bothering to pull on a robe. Unlike Slater. Against her will her eyes were drawn to the open vee between the white lapels of the loosely belted towelling robe he wore, her pulses thudding out an unmistakable message to her.

The robe stopped short at Slater's knees, the unmistakable shape of his hard thighs easily distinguishable beneath the fabric as he came towards her, ushering her out of the room, and then swiftly closing the bedroom door after them.

'What happened?' Chris asked him in a distressed voice. 'I heard the most awful sound . . .'

'Sophie has these nightmares,' he told her in a clipped tone. 'It's the only time she ever uses her vocal chords. They *had* been getting more infrequent.'

The inference was that somehow she was responsible for their re-appearance and Chris flushed angrily. She had been so thrilled by the rapport she seemed to have established with the little girl, and now Slater was making her feel guilty, as though in some way she were responsible for Sophie's distress.

'The theory is that in her nightmares Sophie comes face to face with whatever trauma prevents her from speaking. During the day she's able to keep her fears at bay, but at night . . .' he shrugged, pain etching sharp lines alongside his mouth and Chris ached with sympathy for Sophie and her mental agony.

'If she could just talk about it . . .' she

whispered, more to herself than anything else, but Slater caught the words and grimaced sardonically.

'If she could . . . yes all our problems would be solved and Sophie's with them, but unfortunately she can't.'

They had been walking down the passage as they spoke, Chris reluctantly conscious of Slater's proximity as his thigh occasionally brushed against hers. Outside her door she halted, turning to face him, her heart leaping into her throat with a bound that almost suffocated her as she saw the way he was looking at her. The moonlight through her open door had her trapped in its beam, tracing the outline of her body beneath the thin cotton of her nightdress in faithful detail. She held her breath as Slater's gaze slid slowly over her, trying to quell the tension building up inside her. In the past he had never looked at her like that. He had desired her yes, but he had been conscious of her youth and experience. Now he was studying her with a blend of raw sexual appreciation and contempt that urged her to escape.

'That's a very fetching garment you're wearing,' he drawled softly at last. 'Are you sure you got up purely on Sophie's account, Chris?'

'What do you mean?' The breath hissed from her lungs with the question, her skin colouring with anger as she interpreted his question.

'Oh come on Chris,' he continued, watching her, 'I may not be a member of the jet set crowd you hang around with but I am well aware of the kind of woman you are. Quite a challenge I should imagine, to see if you could come back and take up where you left off, but I'm afraid your reputation's gone to your head my dear I . . .'

Too furious to guard her tongue, Chris interrupted him. 'You know nothing of the woman I am, Slater.' She virtually spat the words at him, her eyes gleaming bright green in the moonlight, her smooth skin flushing with the onrush of adrenalin to her veins. 'And as for what you're implying, I wouldn't touch you if you were the last man on earth. You do nothing for me,' she hurled at him recklessly for good measure. 'You never have and you never will.'

'Oh no?' His fingers gripped her wrist as she reached for the door, imprisoning it almost painfully. He was close enough now for her to be aware of the angry rise and fall of his chest, and of the dark fury burning his eyes to molten amber. 'It's high time someone shook that pedestal you've place yourself on lady,' he ground out against her ear as he bundled her into her room. The moment they were inside, Chris turned on him, reacting instinctively to the fear racing through her, darting for the door as she sought to evade the punishment she sensed he had in mind, but he was too fast for her, leaning against the closed door as she raced for it and using the impetus of her flight to pull her hard against his body, almost knocking the breath from her lungs. His hand left her wrist to grip her waist. She was trapped between his hands, every angry squirm of her body bringing her into closer contact with his unyielding hardness. She could almost feel the rage vibrating inside him.

'I've waited a long time for this opportunity Chris.' His fury almost stunned her. She was at a loss to understand the reason for it. *She* was the one who had been betrayed; who had been so badly hurt that she had had to completely change her life in order to escape the pain, and even then she had not succeeded. 'You owe me . . .'

'I owe you nothing.' Somehow she managed to bring out the angry denial, all too aware that the increased pressure of Slater's hands was forcing her breasts against his chest, the roughly angry movements of his breathing exerting a sensual stimulation that hardened her nipples into provocative invitation and increased her pulse rate. Why was she reacting to him like this when so many other men had left her cold?

Why? Because quite simply her body had never forgotten his touch; had never forgotten the promise implicit in his lovemaking; once long ago she had been programmed to react passionately to his touch, and she was no more able to stop what was happening to her than she was able to understand his motivation.

'Like hell.' He almost snarled the words into her mouth as he bent his head towards her. 'When you left here, you were still a virgin—one of the biggest mistakes I ever made. You won't fool me so easily again Chris.'

Her virginity, that was what he believed she owed him? That was what this was all about? In Slater's eyes she was the one who got away and he bitterly resented that fact. Wasn't he content with the fact that he had seduced her cousin and impregnated her with his child? Was his conceit so colossal that he regretted that she had not shared Natalie's fate?

Hard on the heels of wrenching pain came fierce

rage . . . rage against herself because he could still arouse her, and rage against him, because he was so much less than she had once thought him to be.

'Is that what all this is about Slater?' She marvelled at her own ability to appear cool and mocking. He was angry, dangerously so, and somehow she must get him out of her room before his control broke completely. To wound him where he was most vulnerable—in his outsize ego —seemed her best chance she decided quickly, knowing that she could not trust herself to react logically while he still held her in his arms. That was the bitterest pill of all—despite everything she knew; all the pain she had endured; she was still physically very much aware of him; her body still yearned for him, and she knew that she would have to fight not just him, but her physical craving for him as well.

'My virginity?' She forced a mocking smile. 'It's long gone I'm afraid.'

'And I'll bet you can't even remember the man you gave it to.' There was a bitter violence in his voice; that shook her, alerting her to her increasing danger. 'What can you remember Chris? This?'

His mouth was on hers before she could escape, searing her skin, moulding her lips to the hard contours of his, his tongue expertly prising its way past their soft barrier. A thousand sensations coursed through her veins, chief of which was the knowledge that no man had ever made her feel like this. She knew she should fight to escape, but her body was too weak to obey her mind. She made a soft sound of need in her throat, instantly translated by Slater, his teeth nipping erotically at her skin until her mouth opened, and her hands of their own volition locked behind his head, her fingers clutching at the thick darkness of his hair, as she gave herself up completely to the overpowering rage of need pouring through her. It was as though her starved senses had suddenly come to life, drinking greedily from Slater's mouth, responding to his kiss with a feverish intensity that blotted out all ability to think. His thumb stroked her throat, finding the spot where the soft sounds of pleasure reverberated against her skin, making her tremble with desire.

Her hands slid from his neck to the open lapels of his robe, investigating the powerful structure of his shoulders, his skin warmly sensual like raw silk, to her touch.

She wanted to touch him all over, to absorb him into her and be absorbed by him. It seemed impossible that she could get close enough to him, and his probing thumb registered the impatience of her softly moaned need, as it stroked her throat.

Which one of them loosened the belt of his robe Chris did not know, but she did know that it was Slater who slid the straps of her nightdress down her arms, until the bodice came free, his body taut with desire as he studied the moon-silvered outlines of her breasts. No man had seen her like this before, not even Slater himself, but there was pride in the way Chris held her body, her breathing quickening as she felt Slater register the burgeoning evidence of her desire as her nipples stiffened into hard peaks and she swayed close to him.

Still leaning on the door he pulled her into the cradle of his hips, the hard evidence of his desire for her something that would have shocked her normally but which now made her ache with excitement and need. Rational thought was impossible. Past and present merged and mingled until they were inseparable. The six long years they had been apart might never have been; Chris's body rejoiced in his familiar touch, her mouth pressing wildly pleading kisses against his skin as his hands cupped her breasts and his dark head descended, his lips making a leisurely exploration of her satin skin.

Neither of them spoke a word, the sound of their mingled breathing the only thing to break the thick silence. Obeying some unspoken command Chris arched back against the support of Slater's hands low on her back. In the moonlight her breasts gleamed milky white, their full curves taut and provocative. Her heart thudded with sledge-hammer blows, an aching need coiling in the pit of her stomach. Against her lower body Slater's thighs felt hard and tense, the heat coming off his skin invading her bloodstream and quickening the course of her blood.

One hand left her back to cup her breast, his thumb stroking slowly over the hard peak of her nipple. Slater's gaze fastened on the flesh he was caressing with a tense absorption that tightened the spiral of need inside Chris, until she wanted to cry out with the agony of it.

With almost unbearable slowness Slater lowered his mouth to her breast, stroking agonising deliberate circles of pleasure round the pale skin just beyond the aureole of her nipple. It was a torment Chris couldn't endure. She lifted her hands to his neck burying her fingers in his hair as she urged his mouth against her body, arching it wantonly against him. Still he continued his sensual play with her nipple, teasing it with light moist strokes that drove her into a mindless frenzy of need, husky sounds of frustration joining the growing tension of their breathing.

'Chris . . .' The hoarse sound of Slater's voice intruded on her private world of fantasy, shocking her into reality. Slater raised his head to study her, his eyes missing nothing as they slid slowly over her body in sardonic appraisal of its arousal. The heat inside her turned to ice, and Chris shivered, bitterly regretting her lack of self control.

'What was that you said about me doing nothing for you?'

It was a taunt she might have expected, and one that was well deserved in the circumstances, and where she had ached with desire Chris now ached with pain. As Slater released her, she made an instinctive move to cross her arms over her naked breasts. His expression grimly contemptuous he followed the movement.

'All these years I've wondered what it would have been like with you but a woman who's so easily aroused by every man who touches her is like flat champagne—tasteless and unappetising.'

'You wanted me.' Chris murmured the words in bewildered agony unable to comprehend fully what had happened.

'That was merely a male manifestation of physical desire . . . there was nothing personal in it Chris, just as there was nothing personal in your desire for me. Your New York studs might not mind being merely one of a crowd, but I'm afraid that's not for me.' He opened the door and walked through it leaving her staring numbly after him.

How had it happened? How had he trapped her into betraying herself to him in such a way? Her mind circled endlessly trying to find an explanation, but there was none. Her lips were dry, and she touched them with the tip of her tongue, disturbed by their faintly swollen contours. Like an automaton she pulled on her nightdress, shuddering as deep spasms of self disgust wracked her. She deserved every ounce of the contempt Slater had shown her—not because she was the shallow, self indulgent creature he believed, but because she had allowed her body to betray her mind, to overrule six years of hard work. Originally when she left Little Martin she had told herself that at least she had her self respect; that that was still intact; now she didn't even have that. She had melted in Slater's arms like a lighted candle, like over-dry kindling, and it still shocked her that he had the power to ignite her senses in that way. Viewed from a distance of six years, her adolescent hunger for him had been something she had set aside as unable to happen to her a second time. The intensity of need he could arouse inside her was something she found hard to come to terms with. She knew herself well enough to know that she had never felt like that with anyone else. Slater was the only one who could make her burn with physical hunger. Why? Because of what had happened between them in the past; that must be the answer. Unbidden, another and more serious explanation raised its head, but Chris refused to even admit it. Still in love with Slater? How could she be.

She couldn't hide herself away in her room for

ever, Chris told herself sardonically, studying her
reflection in the mirror, her make-up was flawless,
and only an expert could tell how much she had
done to conceal the results of her sleepless night.
Her hair she had drawn back in a sophisticated
knot; her silk separates were specially chosen to
enhance her cool, touch me not appearance. It was
a little too late to hide behind that façade now, she
told herself cynically, but she needed the armour
of appearing to be in control when she faced
Slater. Her face coloured faintly beneath her
make-up as she remembered her abandoned
response to him. No, Slater wasn't going to allow
her to forget last night in a hurry. Teeth clenched
she walked towards her door. She would *have* to
face him, for Sophie's sake if nothing else.

He lifted his head briefly in acknowledgement of
her presence as she walked into the breakfast
room. Dressed for the office, he looked remote
and formidable. Trying to stem her inward
quivering Chris pulled out a chair and sat down.

'Very impressive.' The paper was laid aside as he
studied her immaculate face and silk blouse. 'But it
doesn't fool me Chris. I ought to thank you for
last night. It might have taken six years to bring
me to my senses, but last night certainly did the
trick. There's nothing like a cold dose of reality for
banishing impossible dreams is there?'

He was talking in riddles that Chris could not
understand. She started to pour herself a cup of
coffee and then stopped as her hand started to
shake.

'Withdrawal symptoms?' His smile was tauntingly cruel. 'You don't have to stay here Chris,
you know that. You can leave any time you like.'

'That's just what you'd like me to do isn't it.' The truth hit her in a blinding flash. Slater was too clever to openly defy Natalie's will, but there were more subtle ways of making sure she never fulfilled her responsibilities towards Sophie. 'I'm not leaving here yet Slater,' she told him curtly, 'Not until I find out what's haunting Sophie . . .'

'Noble sentiments.' His face looked austere, his expression shuttered. 'You realise of course, that we might never find out. Sophie's trauma could be permanent.'

It was a shocking thought. Chris's mind switched from her own problems to the little girl's. 'How is she this morning?' she queried worriedly.

'Still sleeping. She often does after a bad night like last night. I've given Mrs Lancaster instructions to let her sleep on. What do you propose to do with yourself this morning?'

Who did he think he was, her gaoler? Chris frowned deeply. 'I thought I'd go into the village and see about getting the Mini fixed. I can't keep on using someone else's car.'

'Umm . . .'

He didn't speak again until he got up to leave, by which time Chris's nerves were in shreds. Unlike her he seemed to have suffered no after effects from last night, but then unlike her he had not suffered the most acute mental and physical anguish because of it. The most unpalatable thing of all was that her body still ached for him; still hungered for his possession.

After he had gone Chris went upstairs to look in on Sophie. The little girl was so peacefully asleep that it seemed impossible to connect her peace now with the torment she had suffered during the night. Slater had told her that Sophie rarely woke up during her nightmares, and that on her doctor's advice he did not mention them to her when she was awake.

Explaining to Mrs Lancaster where she was going, Chris got in her borrowed car and drove down to the village. The small garage looked much sprucer than she remembered it and the young man who came forward to help her seemed eager to please. Quickly Chris outlined her problem.

'I'll certainly go up and have a look at it for you,' he agreed when she had finished. 'Where did you say you were staying?'

When Chris told him, she was surprised to see the dark colour seeping up under his skin. 'You'll be Nat ... that is Mrs James's cousin then?' he blurted out.

'Yes.' She watched him carefully. Obviously he knew Natalie, but then he would. Little Martin was a very small village. He was quite attractive in a fair-headed, boyish way, probably a couple of years her junior Chris deduced, and possibly something of an idealist.

'You knew my cousin?'

He nodded his head, his colour increasing, his head lowering defensively as he answered. 'She brought her car to me for servicing. We got quite friendly.' His face twisted into a bitter smile. 'If she'd taken my advice she might still be alive now. I knew she wasn't happy, but ...' he turned away, and Chris questioned sharply,

'Natalie told you she wasn't happy?'

'We used to go out for a drink occasionally. Her car hadn't been running very well. I couldn't find anything wrong with it, so she suggested we went out for a drive—she thought the fault might show up better. She told me she was very lonely and we got into the habit of going out once or twice a month.' He saw Chris's expression and not knowing what had caused it and that her sardonic grimace was more for her cousin's duplicity than because of his response to it, said defensively, 'It was all quite innocent . . . she just needed someone to talk to . . . I liked her . . . she said that no one here understood her. She was bored, lonely . . . Her husband ignored her; he had other women. The coroner said that she took her own life because she was severely depressed, but it was her husband who was really responsible. If he hadn't neglected her. If he'd loved her as she deserved to be loved.' He turned to Chris, his face drawn in betraying lines of anguish, and Chris recognised in his expression all his hopeless adoration of her cousin and felt pity for him. 'He refused to sleep with her you know, to be a proper husband to her. It started when she was carrying his child. He said she looked repulsive. He broke her heart.'

His revelations were astounding Chris. She didn't know what to believe. Natalie had always had a penchant for embroidering the truth, but she already knew that her cousin and Slater had separate rooms. Had he perhaps regretted his impulsive marriage to her? Had he ever wished that *she* had been the one he had married? But no, she was letting her imagination run away with her now. Slater had never really wanted her. She knew that Natalie had died from an overdose of sleeping pills and she wondered suddenly if the doctor who had prescribed them had realised how dangerously depressed her cousin was.

Having thanked Natalie's young admirer for his offer to check over the Mini, Chris made arrangements to telephone him in a few days' time to see what progress if any had been made. He had, she learned before she took her leave of him, bought the small village business with a small legacy. Had he and Natalie been lovers? Somehow Chris didn't think so. Richard Courtland did not strike her as the type to involve himself with another man's wife on a physical level. No, whatever comfort Natalie had had from him, it had been of a purely emotional nature Chris felt sure.

Before returning to the house she called in at the village chemist in Little Martin, they shared a doctor with three other villages, and old Doctor Goodfellow had never made any secret of his contempt for sleeping tablets and tranquilisers. Chris was nearly sure he would never have prescribed them for Natalie who had always had a tendency towards morbid hypochondria.

On enquiry the chemist told her cheerfully that Doctor Goodfellow had retired, and that they now came under a local Group Practice based in the nearest town. 'It's Doctor Howard who nearly always does the house calls,' he further amplified. 'He lives just outside the village. He used to practice in London, but when his wife became ill they decided to move down here. Shame about her. Only thirty-two and likely to be an invalid for the rest of her life.' He explained to Chris that the doctor's wife suffered from a progressive muscular wasting disease, adding that their three children were now at boarding school. 'Devoted to his kids Doctor Howard is.'

Smiling mechanically Chris left the shop. It wasn't hard to imagine that an overworked doctor, with as many personal problems as Dr Howard apparently had, would prescribe sleeping tablets for someone like Natalie ... possibly hoping to keep her out of his busy surgery.

Chris wondered if it was worth going to see him. She knew that nothing would bring back her cousin, but she couldn't help thinking if she could discover more about *why* she had taken her own life she might find some clue that would help with Sophie.

It was lunchtime when she got back to the house. Sophie picked lacklustrely at her food, looking heavy-eyed and tired. It transpired that it was Mrs Lancaster's afternoon off, and Chris readily agreed to look after the little girl, suggesting that they went out for a walk.

Sophie nodded her head when the question was put to her, and half an hour later the two of them set off along a path Chris remembered from her own childhood. It led across several fields and on to some open ground where gypsies used to camp when Chris was little. At first Sophie seemed quite eager to walk briskly through the fields. The crops were growing well and as they walked Chris talked, not asking for any reply, but trying to monitor Sophie's response to her chatter. It wasn't until they reached the last field that Chris realised the open ground no longer existed. Several houses had been built on it, including a large bungalow whose back garden overlooked the fields. Frowning slightly she was disturbed to discover that Sophie had suddenly gone rigid, her small body very tense.

'Sophie, darling, what is it?' Chris knelt beside her, looking worriedly at her set face. Sophie was staring in the direction of the new development. Puzzled, Chris followed her concentrated attention. There was nothing especially remarkable about the houses; nothing that to her eyes could have given rise to the little girl's intense reaction.

Deciding to take a risk Chris said casually, 'Come on then, let's go and look at those houses, I haven't seen them before.'

She stood up but before she could take a single step forward Sophie tugged on her hand and refused to move. It wasn't until Chris turned round to face the direction they had come in that Sophie consented to walk.

What had been the cause of her sudden tension? Chris wondered if it was worth mentioning the incident to anyone, reluctant to approach Slater in case he thought she was simply using Sophie as an excuse to draw his attention to her. Her face flamed as she thought about the previous night. She tried to dismiss the memories from her mind, but they kept surging back. The intensity of her own physical response still shocked her; even now she could hardly believe that she had actually experienced such an overwhelming need. It was completely out of character. Completely out of the character she had built for herself since leaving home, she amended slightly. The old Chrissie had reacted in much the same way, only then she had not had the experience to recognise the intensity of her desire.

Sophie looked so tired and drained when they got back to the house that Chris suggested a nap. Although she could not speak Sophie had her own way of communicating and her brief nod confirmed to Chris that the little girl was tired.

With Sophie asleep the rest of the afternoon stretched emptily ahead. It was five o'clock. She had no idea what time she could expect Slater back—if indeed he intended to return for dinner. In the old days he had only worked Saturday mornings. She had a strong suspicion that from now on he would be at pains to avoid her. He had made his point; proved how vulnerable to him she was.

Sighing, Chris remembered her promise to go through Natalie's things. She pushed open the door to her cousin's room, letting out her breath in a faint sigh. The decor was typically Natalie, strong and dramatic with lots of rich colours. A bank of wardrobes filled one wall.

An hour later Chris had accumulated several piles of clothes on the floor beside her. The air around her was thick with her cousin's favourite perfume, almost cloyingly so, and Chris moved back to push open the bedroom door. Natalie certainly hadn't stinted herself on clothes, but then wasn't clothes buying a favoured occupation of lonely, bored women? *Had* her cousin been lonely?

A small sound made Chris turn round. Sophie was standing just inside the open door a look of abject horror on her face. When she saw Chris she made a small, inarticulate sound and hurled herself at her, the force of her small body nearly rocking Chris back on her heels.

Instinctively she comforted the little girl, hugging and soothing her. Sophie buried her face against her breast, breathing in deeply, and it was several seconds before Chris realised that the little girl was trying to absorb *her* perfume. Unlike Natalie's it was light and fresh, and Sophie seemed to find it soothing, because she stopped trembling, and allowed Chris to stand up with her in her arms.

She was just walking towards the door with her, when Slater walked in, his eyes a hard, metallic gold. They raked over her furiously as she stood there, a pulse beating sporadically at the side of his jaw.

'What are you doing?'

'Natalie was my cousin.' Chris replied tautly, for some reason not bothering to explain to him that Mrs Lancaster had requested her help. 'Isn't it natural that I should want to know why she should want to end her life?'

'And you hoped to find explanations in here?' His smile was unkindly derisive. 'Natalie spent almost as little time in her own bed as she did in mine. Well,' he demanded savagely when she stared mutely at him, 'isn't that what you wanted to know? Isn't that one of the reasons why you came back? To see just what havoc you wrought?'

His meaning was lost to her, all she could do was take in the fact that whilst she had assumed Slater's indifference had driven Natalie away from him, he was implying that her cousin had never enjoyed being his wife. What was the truth?

CHAPTER FIVE

NOT wanting to meet Sarah again Chris decided the next time the other girl was due that she would spend the morning at the cottage. Before she got estimates for the work that would need to be done she wanted to have another look at the place. Was it simply misplaced nostalgia that made her want to keep it? After all she was rarely in England these days. Still she wouldn't model for ever, she reminded herself and then there was Sophie. The cottage would be a useful base from which she could see the little girl in years to come. She had a sudden and sharply painful vision of Slater with Sarah and perhaps even their children, herself condemned always to be an outsider in his life, tolerated because Natalie had appointed her as her child's guardian. A bitter thought struck her. Natalie had known how desperately in love with Slater she had been; had her cousin appointed her as Sophie's guardian through some Machiavellian desire to cause her further pain? She frowned, trying to dismiss the thought as she drove towards the cottage. She had heard so much that was conflicting recently, it was no wonder she found it difficult to correlate all the facts properly. For instance Richard had claimed that it had been Slater who rejected Natalie because of her pregnancy, while Slater had implied, without saying as much, that Natalie had been promiscuous—unfaithful to her marriage vows, but then

might her emotionally unstable cousin have
thought she had good reason to be if Richard was
right and Slater had rejected her?

When she pulled up outside the cottage Chris
was no nearer to discovering exactly what she
thought. As a teenager she had found Slater
sexually over-powering; he was a man with a
strong sex drive as recent events had proved and
she couldn't see him absenting himself from his
wife's bed unless there was someone else to take
her place. Had he perhaps betrayed Natalie in the
same way that he had betrayed *her*? Both of them
had been young and innocent—perhaps too naïve
to hold his interest once the thrill of the initial
chase was over.

In the bright early summer sunshine the cottage
looked depressingly delapidated. It would cost a
fortune to put it in order, Chris mused as she
examined the downstairs rooms. The kitchen,
always small and poky needed completely gutting
and perhaps even extending, if planning permission
could be obtained. The prospect of all the work
and expense involved should have been daunting
but as she wandered round Chris found herself
imagining how the cottage could be; how much
she would enjoy being here, looking after Sophie
. . . the two them spending long evenings talking . . . If Sophie ever did talk again.

She must, Chris thought fiercely, somehow the
little girl must be freed from the trauma trapping
her in her world of silence. If only there was some
way she could really help her. The impotence of
her situation galled her. She wanted so much to
help Sophie, already drawn to the little girl in a
way she had never expected. Sophie had much of

her grandmother in her Chris acknowledged; and that combined with the physical similarity between them had forged an almost instantaneous bond. Soberly she reflected on how that same combination must have affected Natalie, who had loathed *her*, and never truly appreciated her own mother.

Sighing Chris made her way upstairs. The stairs creaked protestingly under the pressure of her weight, the banister rail dangerously rickety. Upstairs Chris made instinctively for her own room, her eyes glancing along the familiar book shelves. There were several small gaps. Did that mean that Sophie had more books that had belonged to her? But how had she got them? Chris couldn't see Natalie giving them to her. Natalie had never been a keen reader; indeed Chris had a vivid memory of crying wretchedly under the bedclothes one night because Natalie had mutilated one of her favourite books. Natalie had taken a spiteful pleasure in her distress, she remembered wryly. Could her cousin have changed so much that she had actually wanted to hand Sophie into her care through genuine cousinly love? Chris did not think so. She bit her lip as she stared sightlessly out of the bedroom window. She had a strong conviction that her earlier suspicions had been the right ones. Natalie had made the appointment through sheer malice, knowing how much it would torture her to have to come in close contact with Slater. Knowing . . .

Chris drew in a sharp breath, trembling as she sank down on to her bed, unaware of the damp seeping from it into her jeans. What was she thinking? What was she admitting? Suddenly she had been brought face to face with something she had tried to conceal from herself for years. There had been no one else in her life simply because she had never completely evicted Slater from it. Oh yes, she had gone away, built a new life for herself, but it had been in many ways a sterile life; and no matter how much she tried to deny it to herself she was still very vulnerable to Slater. She had met many men during her career as a model—some as sexually powerful, many better looking, but none of them affected her in the way that he did. She still loved him; if love, such a simple word, was the right description from the frightening complexity and range of emotions he aroused inside her; anger; need; pain, sharply acute sexual hunger, and always a terrible aching loss that she should care so much and he should care not at all.

Shivering, she stood up, pacing the small room, angry with herself and bitterly resentful of Natalie who had forced this confrontation upon her. The other night when Slater had touched her she had responded blindly, instinctively, her starved senses responding to his touch against her will. He believing her to be sexually experienced had put her response down to sexual hunger—she knew better. Wrapping her arms round her slender waist she told herself that Slater must never, ever discover the truth. If he did he would use it to humiliate and degrade her, to mock her and cause her pain as he had done once before. Like a child burned by fire Chris shrank away from even the thought of such pain, remembering how searing and agonising it had been.

Suddenly the cottage seemed claustrophobic. She walked towards the door, bumping into a small chest in her haste. The impact jarred her hip

painfully. It also moved the small chest a few
inches and revealed a man's tie lying half
concealed beneath it. Idly Chris bent and picked it
up. The tie was very traditional; striped in the
fashion of an old school or university tie. She
fingered it absently, noting that the fabric was high
quality silk. How had it come to be in this room?
Perhaps it had been Natalie's father's, although
somehow it looked too new. Telling herself that it
didn't matter who it belonged to, she put it on top
of the chest, and headed for the door.

It was time she returned her borrowed car to its
rightful owner and checked up on the Mini's
progress. If nothing could be done with it she
would have to hire another for the duration of her
visit.

A call at the garage elicited the information that
the Mini was being overhauled and that there was
nothing major wrong with it. It would take two
days to fix, Richard told her with a shy smile,
asking if she wanted him to continue with the work.
Chris said that she did, and then drove on to the
small estate agents' office. Harold Davies was
delighted to see her, and asked her out to lunch.
Remembering the work that would need to be
done on the cottage Chris assented. She would be
able to pick his brains as to who she ought to
employ. When she mentioned the car, he brushed
aside her comments. 'Keep it until yours is ready.
My sister won't be back for some time yet.'

'You really are very generous,' Chris thanked
him. 'I don't know how I'm going to repay you.'

'By having lunch with me today and dinner one
night later in the week,' he responded promptly.

They both laughed. Chris recognised his type of

approach, and was amused by it. Harold Davies was a man who would always enjoy having an attractive woman on his arm; if she was socially or publicly prominent, so much the better. When he married, it would be a carefully judged step, possibly to someone who was faintly 'county'. He was a man who would always put his own interests first, but he was pleasant company. Lunching out would be a welcome break from her too intense thoughts, she decided as she followed him out to his car, smiling faintly as she noticed the impressive lines of the new registration BMW, commenting dutifully on it as she slid into the passenger seat.

'A reasonable car is a must in my business,' Harold told her with a smile. 'Helps impress the clients . . .'

He took her to a small country restaurant that was new to her, but obviously very popular to judge from the packed car park. Without being told Chris guessed that it was the local 'in' place.

'This place hasn't been open very long,' Harold told her, confirming her thoughts. 'I sold them the farmhouse—a very enterprising young couple, who specialise in nouvelle cuisine. I think you'll like it.'

Inside Chris was pleased to see that the farmhouse atmosphere had been retained. The cottage had been skilfully renovated to provide a comfortable, but authentic-looking dining room.

The young woman who greeted them was pleasant and charming. Harold introduced her as Sally Webb, explaining that she and her husband ran the restaurant. 'Paul is king of the kitchen,' Sally added with a grin. 'I'm responsible for the buying and the general running of the place.' They chatted for a few minutes, and then went to the bar to order their drinks. By the time they had been served Sally was back to take them to their table. Although busy, the restaurant wasn't overcrowded, and Chris particularly liked the way the other woman went through the menu with them. The selection was quite small, but very varied, and Chris gave her order confident that she was going to enjoy every mouthful.

They were just waiting for their first course, when a tall fair-haired man walked into the restaurant. Broad shouldered, physically, he was very attractive, although Chris had the unmistakable impression that he was under some degree of strain. His blond hair was already streaked with silver, although he couldn't be more than in his late thirties at the most. When he saw Harold he smiled and came quickly towards them.

'John,' Harold greeted him warmly. 'Are you lunching alone?'

'That was my intention,' the other man agreed.

'Well if Chris doesn't mind, why don't you join us?' Harold suggested quickly.

Put like that Chris could hardly have voiced an objection even had she wanted to, but she didn't. Something about the blond-haired man touched her deeply. She had an intuitive sense that he had experienced great pain. Whoever he was, he must be relatively important for Harold to want him to join them, she thought cynically. A prospective client perhaps?

The introduction when it came startled her. 'Chris, meet John,' Harold smiled, 'Dr John Howard. He lives just outside the village . . .'

'Yes . . .' Chris's smile was automatic. 'Yes, I

know . . .' So this was Dr Howard. The same doctor who had prescribed Natalie's sleeping pills apparently. Was that why he looked so strained? He looked a caring man; one who would suffer from the knowledge that one of his patients had used the drugs he had given for aid, to end her life. And then Chris remembered the story of his wife, and her sympathy increased. Instinctly she put herself out to make him feel at ease, tactfully mentioning in conversation that she was Natalie's cousin, and sensing his controlled start.

'A real tragedy,' Harold interrupted, 'and that poor little kid. How is she, Chris?'

'It's hard for me to say. I know so little about these things. What are the chances of her regaining speech?' She put the question directly to John Howard, glad of an opportunity to get a qualified medical opinion.

'It depends.' He had gone very tense; Chris could plainly see the signs of his tension in his clenched hands and white face.

'On what?' Chris persisted. 'Discovering the cause of the original trauma? I'm sure it's connected with Natalie in some way,' she continued. 'My cousin . . .' She broke off, startled as John Howard upset his drink, the fluid pouring stickily over the table. His face was almost as white as the linen, and Chris was shocked by his tension.

He apologised jerkily. Harold was frowning, and Chris summoned every last ounce of her social poise to smooth over the awkward moment. She didn't know why John Howard had knocked over his drink like that, but plainly he had more compelling things on his mind than Sophie's trauma. She talked gaily for several minutes about her life in New York, making Harold laugh and even drawing a faint smile from John, and by the time their food arrived the awkward moment might never have been.

John ordered quickly, refusing a starter. He and Harold obviously moved in the same crowd, and Chris listened to them discussing a local hunt meeting with one ear while her other senses quivered tensely in response to some silent, subtle message. At last, unable to stop herself, she turned her head.

Now it was her turn to lose colour. Slater was seated three tables away, with two other business-suited men and an extremely glamorous brunette. All four of them seemed to be engrossed in discussion but as her glance lingered on Slater's face it was as though she had sent out some silent message to him. He moved, gold eyes taunting green, his mouth twisting derisively as he studied her too-pale face. Still acutely aware of the morning's unpleasant discovery that she loved him Chris was the first to look away, hoping that he had not noticed the sudden betraying flood of colour surging up under her skin.

Who was the brunette? In other circumstances she would have found her instinctive jealousy almost ridiculous, but now she was held fast in its painfully biting grip, torturing herself on its sharp teeth, as she tried to listen to what her table companions were saying instead of watching Slater.

He was like a magnet, drawing her attention back to him time and time again. On several occasions he looked up to find her watching him, and on one the brunette saw her, and smiled.

'Umm, I hadn't realised Slater was here,' Harold commented following her gaze. 'He's got the Chief Executives from Fanchon with him too ... Must be negotiating another contract with them.'

Fanchon, he went on to explain, were a French company in a similar market to Slater's, to whom he occasionally sold various patent rights.

'And the girl?' Chris asked as lightly as she could.

'Slater's secretary,' Harold told her promptly. Chris felt acutely sick. What was the matter with her? Just because the girl was Slater's secretary it did not necessarily mean that they had a sexual relationship as well as a business one. What about Sarah?

What about her, she derided inwardly, with unusual bitterness. Sarah, like herself and Natalie would no doubt have to accustom herself to sharing him.

She was glad when the lunch was over, and so it seemed was John Howard. There was an almost physical air of relief about him as he stood up. She had not, Chris thought regretfully been able to ask him about Natalie. Moved by sudden impulse she reached out to place a restraining hand on his jacket. 'Please...' she asked huskily, 'could I see you some time ... I want to talk to you about Natalie.' Beneath her fingers Chris felt his arm tense. 'I ... I'll call you,' he told her curtly. 'I must go now...'

'He seems to be under a lot of strain,' Chris commented to Harold as they left the restaurant.

'Yes, well of course, his wife is virtually an

invalid. That can't be easy for a man—a normal, healthy man, to live with. Of course he would never divorce her,' he added, 'she comes from an extremely wealthy family. He was in private practice before she became ill; the work he does now can hardly pay as much, and once one has become used to a certain standard of living . . .'

His comments nauseated Chris, but then Harold would think that way, she told herself as they headed back to his office. That, of course, did not mean that John Howard did. He had struck her as far too sensitive and caring a man to jettison his wife when she needed him the most, but then men as a race rarely thought as women did. Women were capable of great sacrifice on behalf of the men they loved, men seldom returned the favour.

When they returned to his office Chris discussed with Harold the work she believed needed doing on the cottage. As she had hoped he knew of several firms who could carry it out and promised to obtain estimates for her.

'So, it could be that we might see a little more of you in the future,' he commented as he walked with her to the car. 'I'm very glad.' Before she left he asked her out to dinner mentioning that some friends of his were holding a twenty-first party for their daughter and that he would like her to accompany him. The party was on Saturday, and Chris asked him if she could let him know. She hadn't come to Little Martin to socialise, but for Sophie's sake, then again though by Saturday she might be glad of an excuse to escape from the house and Slater's disturbing presence.

Sophie was having a nap when Chris got back to the house. Sarah had left but Mrs Lancaster raised her eyebrows when Chris asked what progress had been made. 'Sarah gets too impatient with her. Succeeding with Sophie is very important to her—too important perhaps. I think she hopes to impress Slater . . .'

Chris was a little surprised that the housekeeper should speak to her so freely, but then no doubt Mrs Lancaster, who couldn't know of the events of the past, considered Chris as a member of Slater's family. Had Natalie envisaged how she would feel; how she would suffer being in such close proximity to Slater. She shuddered suddenly. Could that thought perhaps even have been in her cousin's mind in those last moments before her death? All at once she could almost feel Natalie's malevolence reaching out to touch her. Shrugging aside the unpleasant sensation she went upstairs to Sophie's room. The little girl was fast asleep. She had been drawing, and sheets of brightly coloured paper littered the bed. Almost absently Chris started to pick them up, freezing as she studied the stick figures. In one drawing a small stick figure was confronting a larger one, both, to judge from the dresses Sophie had drawn on them, female. The larger one's face was contorted in an expression of anger so violent, Chris could almost feel it. She couldn't see the smaller figure's face because Sophie had drawn her back view. Quite irrationally she felt that the drawing had some relevance to Sophie's trauma, and she riffled through the other drawings, studying them all carefully, but there were none similar.

Extracting the drawing she bent down to touch the sleeping child's hair. Poor Sophie. If only she was *her* child Chris thought achingly, hers and

Slater's. Angry with herself she went into her own room, putting the drawing in the drawer beside her bed. She wanted to show it to Slater, but she was afraid he would dismiss her suspicions as childish.

Restless; pursued by unwelcome thoughts she wandered out into the garden. Beyond the expanse of lawn a winding path led to a secluded summerhouse, built beside an ornamental fish pool. The pool had always entranced Chris; the peace and solitude of the summerhouse drawing her, and she headed there now. Sheltered from the rest of the garden by a screen of trees, it had a secret, ageless air.

The summerhouse was unlocked and Chris walked inside, noticing that since she had last visited it, new cushions had been made for the seats that lined one wall. She had often imagined Edwardian ladies taking afternoon tea here, swinging gently in a hammock beside the pool perhaps, while fanned by some ardent, but bashful admirer. Lost in daydreams, she jumped tensely when she heard Slater's voice, calling her name, her instinctive, 'what are you doing here?' drawing a sardonic smile from his lips. 'I live here,' he drawled, 'What's your excuse?'

She shrugged, striving to steady her racing pulses. 'The summerhouse always drew me.' Too late she recalled with intense clarity that they had once taken shelter here from a sudden summer storm, her thin cotton dress had been soaked in their impulsive instinctive dash for shelter, and she had not realised why Slater was studying her so intently until she looked down and saw the outline of her breasts clearly delineated beneath the thin cotton. That had been the first time he had kissed her with real passion, his hands molding the firm shape of her breasts, teaching her things about her own burgeoning sexuality she had never dreamed possible. With an effort she dragged her thoughts away from the past.

'Enjoy your lunch?'

Slater was watching her, waiting to trap her, she sensed intuitively. 'Very much,' she responded coolly. 'Enjoy yours?'

'Financially it was extremely rewarding, as no doubt was yours. Two new possible lovers discovered in one day, but that's all they'll ever be Chris—lovers. Harold won't marry anyone less than someone with the right social pedigree, and John Howard will never leave his wife. But then you always did have a penchant for other people's men, didn't you? Those were always the sort of men you wanted.'

She could sense his anger without knowing the cause for it. She could feel it reaching out to envelop her like a blast of heat and she responded to it, driven to goad him by saying mockingly. 'I once wanted you Slater . . . remember?'

For a moment the folly of her taunt crystallised in her mind and she wanted to call the words back, but Slater was already reacting, his mouth twisted in a bitter parody of a smile.

'Oh yes, I remember all right . . .' he agreed smoothly. 'I just wish to hell I didn't,' Chris thought she heard him mutter under his breath as he came towards her. 'I remember this.' He reached her before she could evade him, the back of the cushions brushing against the back of her knees as she tried to move away.

'What are you so nervous about, Chris?' he

asked her mockingly. 'Why the timid virgin act? You must have played this scene a thousand times since we first rehearsed it here in this summerhouse. How did it go?' His voice had an ugly taunting sound that tore at her heart. 'Oh yes ... Take one rain-dampened girl ... conveniently not wearing a bra.'

'Stop it.' The words were torn from her throat making it ache with pain. He was deliberately trampling on all her memories, destroying not just her future but her past, turning something that to her at least had been poignantly beautiful into something mundane and even unpleasantly calculated. There had been nothing calculated in her response to him; nor in her embarrassment when she found him looking at her. Her breasts rose and fell in quick agitation beneath her cotton shirt, her breath tightening painfully into an explosive knot in her chest when Slater deliberately placed one hand either side of her head on the wall behind her, leaning his torso towards her.

He was close enough for her to catch the scent of his body, male and slightly musky as though tormenting her like this was something that vaguely excited him. The thought made her nauseous, her body trembling with reaction. She was old enough to be able to handle this situation with sophistication, she reminded herself, so why wasn't she doing so? Why was she reacting like an adolescent, torn between escape and desire.

'Stop it?' His eyebrows rose. 'I haven't even begun to start yet Chris. And besides you don't really want me to stop do you?'

She turned her head away so that she wouldn't have to look at him, shocked when his fingers suddenly bit into her arms, and he hauled her against his body. 'Do you?' he grated, almost shaking her.

'What am I supposed to say Slater?' For a moment she had almost believed the harsh voice held a note of fierce agony, but she dismissed this as sheer imagination, reminding herself of how he had hurt her; of how he must not guess how she felt. Summoning all her courage she threw back her head, forcing herself to meet his eyes. 'What do you want from me Slater? What do you want to hear me say? That I want you?'

'Yes . . . damn you. Yes! You owe me Chris . . .' His voice dropped slightly over the last few words, his eyes dark with anger.

Chris was too stupefied to respond. *She* owed *him*? How could he stand there and expect her to accept that?

'You owe me . . .' He repeated the words as though they were some private incantation as he bent his head, the hard pressure of his body against hers making Chris acutely aware of his arousal. It was all so unexpected and inexplicable that she had no defences against him. The pressure of his mouth was fiercely, angrily demanding, savaging the softness of her lips, invoking a response from her that brought thickly muttered sounds of pleasure from his throat.

She was lost, completely and utterly, Chris thought hazily, melting beneath the heat of his kiss, wanting him . . . loving him. . .

'Slater?'

Sarah's voice from outside the summerhouse broke into the dreamworld Chris had entered. Instinctively she tensed, breaking away from

Slater. He was breathing heavily, the pupils of his eyes dilated, whether by anger or passion Chris could not tell. She was old enough now to know that men did not necessarily love and respect where they desired and she had to turn away as Sarah entered the summerhouse, sickened by her own blind, betraying response to him.

'Oh there you are,' she heard the other girl saying peevishly. 'I've been looking for you. We're supposed to be going out to dinner tonight . . .'

'Yes, I know. What progress have you made with Sophie today?'

If she had needed confirmation that Slater cared nothing for her, she had it in his swift reversion to normal; his complete lack of interest in her.

'Not much.'

Chris forced herself to turn round, shaken by the open hostility in Sarah's eyes as she studied her. 'She seems to be very disturbed by your presence.' She looked directly at Chris. 'If you want my opinion Slater, you'll get rid of her. Sophie will never make any progress while she stays here upsetting her.'

Chris held her breath, almost dizzy with the effort as she waited for Slater to denounce her and agree with Sarah.

'I can't do that,' he astounded her by saying. 'Natalie chose Chris as Sophie's guardian . . .'

'Heaven alone knows why,' Sarah cut in impatiently. 'She never had a good word to say for her while she was alive.' She turned away opening the summerhouse door. 'I'll see you later then Slater . . .'

She went without a word to Chris, who wondered why she had come when she was seeing

Slater later on that evening. Perhaps she wanted to reinforce to Chris her involvement with him. Suddenly she felt very vulnerable and insecure. Perhaps Sarah was right. Perhaps she was having a bad effect on Sophie? Her negative feelings made her murmur softly, 'I don't know why Natalie appointed me either . . .'

The tension emanating from Slater as she made the admission startled her. His face was pale under his tan, the skin drawn tightly over the bones of his face. 'Oh come on, Chris,' he said icily. 'We both know exactly why . . .'

He turned on his heel and left her before she could say another word, but Chris was glad she was alone. The pain of the blow he had just dealt her was so severe that she would have broken down if he'd stayed. He knew . . . He knew how she felt about him and just why Natalie had appointed her. He *knew* and he was adding to her torment deliberately. He must hate her nearly as much as Natalie had!

Instinctively she wanted to escape, to put as much distance between herself and Slater as she could, but she could not do it, for Sophie's sake. She must simply stay and endure.

CHAPTER SIX

THAT night Chris went to bed early, but sleep eluded her. Of course her wakefulness had nothing to do with the fact that Slater was out with Sarah, she derided herself, as she lay tense waiting for the sound of his returning car. All these years she had deluded herself that she was over him; that he meant nothing to her other than bad memories and now in a few short days the protective cover she had built around herself had been blasted away.

Not until she heard Slater's car stop outside the house did she manage to sleep. A glance at her watch showed her that it was nearly two o'clock. Jealousy, fiercely corrosive and painful overwhelmed her as she pictured Sarah in Slater's arms. Her desire to find out why Natalie had taken her own life was fast being overtaken by an instinctive need to get away from Slater before he discovered her truth. His taunt of the early evening haunted her; he knew why Natalie had appointed her Sophie's guardian; he knew exactly how vulnerable she was, but please God he did not know yet *why* she was so vulnerable. If only she could leave, but there was Sophie to consider; Sophie who reached out and touched her heart; Sophie who she sensed needed her. Perhaps she *was* over-dramatising she reflected in the morning as she dressed. Why should Sophie respond to *her* when she did not to Sarah or her own father? She

went from her own room to the little girl's and
found her getting dressed. Her smile when she saw
Chris banished all her doubts, and Chris hugged
her instinctively, tensing as the door opened and
Slater walked in.

He surveyed them with unreadable eyes for
several long seconds. Dressed formally in a
business suit he looked so physically attractive that
Chris felt her stomach actually clench in fierce
desire.

Sophie, unaware of the under-currents flowing
deep and fast between the two adults, beamed at
her father.

'I'm leaving early this morning,' Slater told
Chris when she had transferred Sophie into her
father's arms, 'and I don't expect to be in to
dinner tonight.'

Sarah again? Chris thought jealously. She had
to avert her face so that he wouldn't see what she
was feeling. 'Oh, I nearly forgot,' he added
drawlingly, an expression in his eyes that Chris
could not define, but which made her shudder with
tense dread, 'some mail arrived for you this
morning.'

He reached into his pocket and withdrew a
bundle of envelopes. Chris had left his address as
her forwarding address with her agent and she
took the letters from him in silence. As she did so,
the top envelope slipped sideways. Like most of
the others it carried an air mail sticker. Written
on pale blue paper, on the reverse side was the
sender's name and address and Chris smiled
involuntarily as she reached for it, unaware of how
much her smile changed her expression.

'You're still in touch with Thornton then?'

The harsh contempt in Slater's voice made her stiffen, her head bowed as she retrieved her letter. 'I read that he married . . .'

'Yes . . . He has a little boy now,' Chris told him smoothly, unable to understand the reason for his obvious contempt. She knew that he and Ray had not been particular friends when Ray had lived locally, but she could see no reason for him to react in the manner he was doing.

'You're a very cool lady Chris.' The way he said it, it wasn't a compliment. 'Does his wife . . .' He stopped as the telephone started to ring, putting Sophie down on the floor. 'I'm expecting a call,' he told Chris curtly. 'That will be it.'

When he had gone Sophie looked uncertainly up at her. Just because the little girl could not speak, it did not mean she could not understand, Chris thought guiltily, forcing a smile and reaching out to take Sophie's hand. Her responsive smile made her heart ache. There was something so familiar about it, and yet it wasn't Slater's smile, she realised, with a small stabbing shock, and it certainly wasn't Natalie's. It must be Sophie's resemblance to herself that she saw in her smile Chris reflected, and yet something tugged at her memory, something elusive that she knew she should remember, but could not.

She read Ray's letter over breakfast. It was teasingly chatty and included an invitation to visit them later in the year. It was high time she learned to stop leaning on Ray and Dinah she thought wryly as she put it back in its envelope and then turned to study the photographs he had sent her. Both of them were of Dinah his wife, and Jeremy, now nearly three years old. The toddler beamed out of the photograph, and sensing Sophie's curiosity Chris showed it to the little girl.

'My that's a bonny little boy,' Mrs Lancaster commented, coming in with their breakfast, and glancing over Chris's shoulder, she put her head on one side, and ruminated, 'Reminds me of someone, but I can't just think who for the moment.'

'His father used to live locally,' Chris offered, 'and Jeremy is very like him facially, although he has his mother's colouring.'

They chatted for a while and then Chris offered to take Sophie out into the garden so that Mrs Lancaster could get on with her work.

Chris had brought some more books back from the cottage and she ran upstairs to get one. Half an hour later, she glanced up from the page she was reading to study Sophie's entranced face. *Winnie the Pooh* was obviously as firm a favourite with Sophie as it had been with her.

'I'll just read to the end of this chapter and then we must stop,' she told her with a smile. She had fallen easily into the habit of talking to Sophie as though she had expected her to respond. The little girl had her own ways of communicating what she wanted or needed, and Chris sighed faintly when she closed the book, wondering if she would ever talk again.

'Time for my exercises,' she told Sophie, standing up. 'Want to watch?'

As a model her exercise regime was an integral part of Chris's life, and when Sophie nodded her head she held out her hand to her. 'Come on then. We'll do them outside today as it's so nice. Let's go upstairs and get my cassette.'

While Chris changed into shorts and a brief top Sophie watched her gravely. An idea suddenly occurred to Chris. 'You can do them with me this morning,' she told her with a smile. 'Let's go and find your shorts shall we?'

When Sophie made no demur Chris took her into her bedroom and helped her to change into shorts and a tee-shirt.

Outside in the garden, she did a few basic warm up exercises and then turned to Sophie, showing her a simpler easy version that would not tax her growing muscles. To her delight Sophie responded enthusiastically. She had a natural physical rhythm that helped her adapt quickly to the exercise routine. Chris had deliberately opted for a 'fun' tape with lively music including several 'pop' songs that had recently been in the charts. She could miss out on serious exercises for one day, and the physical fun of joining in with her would be good for Sophie she was sure. The child must feel the effect of all the adult concern concentrated on her.

They were halfway through the tape when Chris suddenly became aware of a sound other than that issuing from the tape which was playing a popular hit tune. Hardly daring to believe what she was hearing she kept on moving automatically, edging slightly closer to Sophie. Disbelief made her heart turn over with joy as she discovered that she was right, Sophie was actually humming in time to the song. Chris didn't know what to do. One part of her wanted to hug the little girl and show her excitement and yet another warned her that Sophie's humming was entirely spontaneous, something she herself was probably not even aware of and that to draw attention to it might cause all sorts of repercussions. Suddenly she wished she knew more about Sophie's condition; that she could help her; but not daring to do anything she simply carried on with her exercises, trying not to let Sophie sense her excitement.

She didn't hum with any other songs, and afterwards, thinking about it, Chris realised that that particular tune had been in the hit parade for some weeks prior to Natalie's death. Could there be any connection? She *had* to talk to someone. Slater was unobtainable; Sarah she couldn't bring herself to contact, so that left who? Suddenly she thought of John Howard. *He* lived locally, so surely he must be in the telephone directory.

Telling herself that he probably wouldn't even be at home, Chris nevertheless found his number and dialled it, her heart thudding with tremulous excitement.

To her relief he actually answered the 'phone. Quickly Chris announced herself. 'I was wondering if you could come over,' she told him breathlessly. 'It's about Sophie ... the most curious thing ... I thought I heard her actually humming just now ...' She held her breath dreading hearing him scorn her discovery, but to her pleasure he seemed almost as excited as she was. 'I'll be over right away,' he told her.

Replacing the receiver, Chris went in search of Mrs Lancaster. 'I'm expecting Dr Howard soon,' she told the older woman, surprised when she frowned and looked rather disapproving.

'Is something wrong?' she questioned uncertainly. 'I ..., wanted to talk to him about Sophie ...' Quickly she explained what had happened in the garden and at once Mrs Lancaster's expression lightened.

'He'll certainly be the best person to talk to,' she told Chris. 'Used to specialise in children's ailments before he came down here. Said it took up too much of his time.'

'Yes. I can understand that he'd want to spend as much time as he can with his wife,' Chris commented. 'It must be dreadful for her, poor woman . . .'

'Aye, but there's them as thinks it's worse for him,' Mrs Lancaster told her obliquely, 'being tied to an invalid and all . . . Of course she's secure enough. He couldn't divorce her. He only works part-time now and it's her money that supports them. Comes from a very wealthy family. Her father was extremely well to do and she was the only child . . .'

'Oh I'm sure that isn't the reason he stays with her,' Chris was extremely distressed by Mrs Lancaster's comment although she couldn't exactly say why. Perhaps it was because she had suffered so much disillusionment herself that she couldn't bear to hear of any male betrayal of her sex.

'Maybe not.' Mrs Lancaster's voice was non-committal but the smile she gave Chris extremely warm.

She was just going upstairs to change when the 'phone rang in the hall. She picked up the receiver, surprised to hear an unfamiliar female voice.

'I'm Helen Howard,' she introduced herself. 'My husband asked me to give you a call. He was just on his way round when he was called out to an emergency—a road accident. He'll be with you as soon as he can. How is Sophie?' she asked in concern. 'She was always such a warm, responsive child, I hate to think of her suffering . . .'

As *she* suffered, Chris thought intuitively, liking the other woman without knowing her. They chatted for several minutes and then Chris hung up, retracing her footsteps to the kitchen to advise Mrs Lancaster of the changed arrangements.

It was after lunch before John Howard finally arrived. Chris was sunbathing in the garden, Sophie asleep beside her.

'Sorry I couldn't get here sooner,' he apologised.

He looked tired, Chris realised, getting up carefully so that she didn't disturb Sophie. 'That's all right,' she told him easily. 'Your wife explained when she rang.'

Something flickered in his eyes and was gone. Pain possibly Chris decided, suddenly aware of how healthy she must appear in contrast to Helen.

'Beautiful day.' He shrugged off his jacket and grimaced. 'That's better.' He was formally dressed, wearing a stiped tie that was vaguely familiar Chris realised, mentally comparing it to the one she had picked up in the cottage. Were they the same? She shrugged aside the thought as unimportant and improbable. What would one of John Howard's ties be doing in her aunt's cottage?

'I'll go and make us some coffee,' Chris offered, picking up her robe and tying it. There was nothing indecent about her bikini but nevertheless she felt better a little more covered up.

When she returned with the coffee and some lemonade for Sophie the little girl was still asleep. Encouraged by John Howard she explained what had happened that morning.

'Umm, as you describe it, it sounds like a

completely involuntary thing—if nothing else it proves conclusively that there's no damage to the vocal chords, but then we never thought there was. Was Sophie herself aware of what she was doing?'

Chris shook her head. 'I didn't dare to draw attention to it. Should I . . .'

He shook his head anticipating her question. 'No . . . no you did the right thing. Does Sophie have her own tape or radio?'

When she shook her head, he mused, 'It might be an idea to get her one. If we can get her to respond to music it will help . . .' He broke off as Sophie woke up, lifting her head. Chris smiled at her, worried by the look of total terror she suddenly saw in the little girl's eyes. As she picked her up she could feel the waves of tension shuddering through her body, but was at a loss to understand the reason for them. 'What is it, darling?' she asked softly. 'Did you have a bad dream?'

'Something wrong?' John Howard looked ill at ease.

'She seems terrified of something,' Chris told him. 'Perhaps she's been having a bad dream.'

'Is that what it was, Sophie?' He reached out a hand and Chris was almost overbalanced by the force with which Sophie drew away from him, clinging to her and turning her head into her shoulder. John Howard's hand dropped away. 'It seems she doesn't much care for me,' he said wryly. 'Poor Sophie, I suspect she's grown very wary of all us medical types, and perhaps it's no wonder.' He made no further effort to touch the little girl, and Chris was warmed by the expression of guilt and unhappiness in his eyes. He obviously

cared very deeply about his patients, but she could
understand that Sophie might distrust and perhaps
even dislike the medical profession as a body.

'Why don't you go upstairs and choose a book
for me to read from?' she suggested softly, putting
Sophie down. 'Dr Howard is just going . . .'

They both watched her run away. 'I'm sorry she
reacted to you like that,' she apologised ruefully,
'but . . .'

'*You're* sorry?' His expression almost agonised
he gripped her forearms, his face contorted with
pain. 'Chris there's . . .' He broke off turning to
look towards the drive as they both heard the
sound of a car.

'Slater,' Chris murmured frowning. 'But he
said he wouldn't be coming home until after
dinner.' She could still sense John Howard's
tension and as Slater stopped the car and
climbed out, she reached up instinctively to
touch his face in a gesture of commiseration, her
smile warmly sympathetic. 'It must be difficult
for you,' she said understandingly, 'but . . .' She
had intended to go on to say that he must be
used to his small patients reacting against him
when they had to endure pain and suffering, but
his tortured, 'Difficult—my God . . .' stopped
her. Unaware of how close they were to one
another, or how their proximity might appear to
an onlooker, it took Slater's harsh exclamation
to make her step back involuntarily, her nerves
tensing in response to his nearness.

Dimly she was aware of John Howard saying
goodbye, and something about getting in touch
with her, as he hurried away, her senses totally
concentrated on Slater.

'You said you weren't coming back until after dinner.'

Stupidly she had made the words sound like an accusation, and Slater's mouth hardened. 'This *does* happen to be my home,' he ground out bitterly, 'and I won't have you tainting it by filling it with your lovers. What's the matter, Chris?' he demanded thickly when she simply stared at him, totally non-plussed by his accusation. 'Came back at the wrong moment did I ... Your body still aches for completion, does it? Well I might not be John Howard but I reckon I can satisfy you as well as he could ...'

'No ...' The panic-stricken word was clawed from her throat.

'Yes ...'

She had always known that Slater was strong, but how strong she had not realised until he picked her up, clamping hard arms round her, carrying her over the grass despite her desperate attempts to escape. He was heading for the summerhouse, she realised dazedly gasping as he opened the door and slid her to her feet, securing her wrist with one hand, while the other deftly locked the door. She tried to escape, using her nails on his hand to try and prise them free, but apart from a brief grunt of pain there was no response. Red weals lined his tanned skin, his expression savage as he followed her glance down to them.

'My God I'll make you pay for that,' he muttered thickly, and Chris wondered fearfully if he was temporarily deranged. There was no smell of drink on his breath, and in most respects he appeared completely normal, but there was nothing normal about the way he had dragged her in here, locking the door behind them and then pocketing the key. Neither was there anything normal about the way he was watching her, the gold eyes dilated, burning with a fever that was mirrored in the dark surge of colour running up under his tanned skin. He was almost savage with rage, Chris acknowledged, shuddering deeply. He reminded her of a wild animal penned up in a cage, secured for the time being but relentlessly determined to escape, infinitely dangerous in his captivity. What was it that held Slater in captivity? The memory of Natalie? Was that why he was here? Did he share her cousin's hatred of her? Was this his way of showing his grief? A sacrifice of her on the altar of his guilt towards Natalie?

His relationship with her cousin had obviously been particularly complex, if *he* was to be believed at least ... but they had stayed married, and he had tolerated her infidelities.

'Is that what you like, Chrissie?' His voice was almost hypnotic. The purr of the jungle panther before it tore out its victim's throat Chris thought trembling. 'Sex mixed with violence? Is that what excites you ... drawing blood physically as well as mentally?'

His words seared through her, shocking her and making her ache with renewed pain. This was not the Slater she had cherished in her memories; the lover she had dreamed of at night, even though in the morning she had managed to deny those dreams to herself.

'What I *don't* like is being forced against my will, Slater.' She managed to utter the words with some semblance of self-assurance, using her model's poise to conceal her fear. 'If you just unlock that door, I'll forget this even happened . . . If not . . .'

'If not, you'll what?' he jeered bitterly. 'Cry rape?'

The jibe stabbed right through her body, making her tense in shock and anger, the ugliness of the word bringing a hideous reality to her situation.

'Oh no,' Slater muttered savagely. 'It won't be rape, Chrissie . . . that wanton body of yours is going to want me just as much as it wanted John Howard. Funny about you and Natalie, how you always wanted the same man . . .'

The cruel taunt robbed her of the ability to speak. She hated him for choosing now to remind her of her vulnerability to him. Of course he felt confident that he could make her want him. He knew how she had responded to him in the past. What she couldn't understand was why he thought she had even contemplated making love with John Howard but that hardly mattered now. Somehow she was going to prove to him that she could resist him and that would take every ounce of willpower she possessed.

As he came towards her she refused to move, even though every nerve in her body cried out for her to back away. Her best form of protection was cold rejection. Flight would only increase his belief that he could subdue her.

His hands untying the knot of her robe and then sliding up over her body were a shocking reality. Fiercely keeping her face averted, Chris willed herself not to react. She was simply posing for an ad, she told herself frantically, Slater's hands were

simply those of another model ... But no other
man had ever touched her like this, and her body
refused to accept her deception. She shuddered as
Slater's fingers bit into her shoulders. 'I think we
can dispense with this,' he told her softly, adding
mockingly. 'Why are you shivering, Chrissie? You
can't possibly be cold.'

If anything the summerhouse was over-warm,
and his mockery broke through the façade of her
control. 'Don't call me that,' she demanded
huskily, referring to his special use of her name.

'Why not? You used to like it ... I was the only
person who called you Chrissie, you once told me,
and you said just hearing my voice saying your
name brought you out in goosebumps.'

She had said that, Chris remembered achingly,
and although he had laughed gently at her naïveté
she remembered that always after that when they
were alone Slater would murmur her name against
her skin, savouring her instantaneous response to
him.

His hands slid the robe off her shoulders and
much as she would have liked to have fought to
retain it, Chris let it go. It would be undignified to
struggle she told herself, and besides the best way
of resisting him was simply not to respond. Her
bikini wasn't particularly brief by modern standards, but she felt acutely uncomfortable as Slater
studied her.

'You always did have a beautiful body,
Chrissie.' He murmured the words against the
vulnerable skin of her throat. Chris gritted her
teeth together, willing herself not to respond, and
hating Slater with a wave of feeling so strong that
it dizzied her as he laughed gently, his thumb

registering the hurried thud of her pulse, his mouth, moving with unerring precision against her skin, closer and closer to the base of her throat.

Wild surges of desire tormented her, every instinct urging her response. It was so tempting simply to arch her throat against his mouth; to curl her fingers into his hair and hold him locked against her while her heated blood pounded out its message against his lips, but she wasn't going to give in.

'Still the same old Chrissie.' His mouth left her skin, but his thumb continued to torment the thudding pulse. 'Ready to cut your nose off to spite your face. You know you want me, and I know it too ...'

'I don't.' The hot denial was out before she could silence it, temper glittering greenly in her eyes. To her surprise Slater laughed, a rich, triumphant sound that skittered dangerously over her taut nerves. 'Now that's better. Real emotion at last. You're lying, Chris,' he added sleekly. 'You want me all right. I can see it here.' His thumb touched her pulsing throat, in a tormenting caress that forced her to smother an aching groan. 'And here.'

His hand moved, and Chris closed her eyes in fierce pain as his thumb moved with insolent appraisal over the hardening nub of one breast. She didn't want to open her eyes but something forced her to do so. She didn't want to look down at Slater's lean brown hand where it rested against the underside of her breast, but she felt impelled to. Against the thin cotton of her bikini top her nipples strained in unmistakable arousal, panic clawing in the pit of her stomach, mingling with her aching muscles until she felt she would snap in two with the tension.

'You want me,' Slater insisted thickly, 'and although I'll probably be damned for it, I *ache* for you.'

'No . . .' Her wild moan of denial seemed to unleash something deeply primitive inside him, because Slater's restraint snapped and he pulled her fiercely against his body, crushing her against his chest, his hand trapping hers against his thigh, forcing her to acknowledge his arousal as he muttered rawly. 'Yes . . . Yes . . . Chris . . . Feel how much I want you, and you want me the same way . . . I know you do.'

It was useless to keep on resisting him. The heat of his body beneath her hand in those few seconds before he had let her pull away had left her with a suffocating emotional response. She was a fool to be swayed simply by his desire for her; hadn't she learned just how little male desire really meant? And yet the knowledge of his need for her touched off something elemental buried deep inside her that once awakened could not be subdued.

She was barely aware of her own soft moan as Slater untied her bikini top, her senses all too attuned to him; to the hurried rise and fall of his breathing; the darkening glitter of his eyes as he pushed her away from him to study the full perfection of her breasts. Heat rose up in a dark tide under his skin. He thrust off his jacket, wrenching impatiently at his tie, and as though the impatience of his movements were an echo of her own feelings Chris felt the surge of desire sweep tormentingly through her body, inducing a yearning ache in her lower stomach and making her breasts swell, her nipples rosily erect.

Chris had never posed for any photographs that involved her going even topless, never mind nude, and she was torn between shame and excitement as she saw Slater's reaction to her evident arousal, and discovered the sensual pleasure of knowing he was watching her, his body taut with hunger.

He pulled at the top two buttons of his shirt, abandoning the task to take her in his arms, his voice hoarse and muffled against the smooth skin of her shoulder as he demanded. 'Take it off for me, Chrissie. I think I'll go mad if I don't touch you.'

As she made a tentative movement towards the small pearl buttons Chris felt the heat of his skin burning into her through the fine material of his shirt. The need to feel that heat directly against her skin was almost terrifying in its intensity. She didn't know which of them was trembling the most she thought hazily as she tried to work the small buttons free, one hand flat against the hard wall of Slater's chest as she steadied herself. All the time she was trying to concentrate on her task, Slater's mouth was playing delicately over her skin, caressing the line of her neck and shoulder. Shivers of pleasure raced through her, as the last button came free and she tugged the shirt tails free of his waistband. His body was harder; stronger than she remembered, the muscles of his stomach drawn in sharply as her fingernails accidentally grazed against his chest. The hair that grew there was dark, and oddly smooth, and she gave in to the temptation to run her fingertips lightly through it.

Slater's sharp gasp brought her explorations to

a sudden halt, pleasure flooding her body like melted honey as he bit into her skin, pulling her against him so that the fine dark hairs grazed arousingly against her swollen nipples. When he moved, increasing the tormenting contact, Chris moaned huskily in her throat, her mouth finding the hard column of his throat. It arched beneath her tentative caress inciting further exploration. Delicately Chris brushed her thumb over its male outline, feeling Slater's harsh sound of pleasure reverberating beneath her hand. Her lips touched the spot caressed by her thumb and she was startled by the harsh exclamation of sound Slater made, his hand cupping her breast, stroking urgently over its hard tip.

'Chrissie.' The sound of her name was lost beneath the savage pleasure of his kiss, their mouths melding and fusing, passion a tangible force enveloping them as Chris wrapped her arms round him, exulting in the fierce abrasion of his body hair against her breasts, pulsing with feverish need that betrayed itself in the compulsive thrust of her lower body against his as it demanded an increasingly closer contact with the hard muscles of his thighs.

They were still standing up, and when Slater released her breast, his hands moving swiftly down her body, to slide inside the cutaway legs of her bikini bottom, and hold her against him so that she could feel the shudders of need pulsing through him she gloried in the intimate contact, pressing wild kisses against his moist skin. A wildness she hadn't known herself capable of entered her blood, her hands stroking feverishly over Slater's torso, her mouth obedient to Slater's muttered urgings, following a path downward over his throat and shoulder until she rested against the hard, almost flat outline of his nipple.

Shock held Chris almost rigid for a moment, the heat of Slater's hands cupping her bottom sending shivers of intense pleasure quivering through her. His body pulsed frantically against hers one hand freeing itself from her lower body to tangle in her hair and then spread against the back of her head. 'Yes ... Chrissie,' she heard him mutter, as she was convulsed with waves of pleasure. 'Yes ... kiss me ...' Feverish sounds of pleasure wracked his body as she let her lips play with the small hard nub of flesh, and feeling suddenly, recklessly responsive, Chris let her tongue play delicately over his tense skin, teasing it with her lips, until Slater gave a harsh moan that demanded fulfilment of the promise her tormenting mouth implied.

The hoarse, almost feverish words ignited her own passions, her body throbbing with aching need as she stroked and kissed as much of his body as she could.

It was the barrier of his waistband and belt that stopped her—that and the sudden sensation of losing her balance, that it took her several seconds to recognise the fact that Slater had lifted her off her feet and was carrying her over to the low cushioned bench against the wall.

'Chris ... my God, how you torment me.' The thick admission was made as Slater lowered her on to the cushions. Still bending over her, he studied her almost broodingly for a second and Chris shivered lightly under that exploration. She wanted him so much it hurt, and suddenly, she knew that no matter how much she suffered for it afterwards she desperately wanted him to make love to her. It wasn't simply a matter of appeasing her aching body. It was something to hold on to in the lonely future. Something to dream about and to remember. And she always *would* remember that she had aroused him; that she had made him tremble and cry out with a pleasure so fierce that she could still see it beating in his body. Instinctively she knew that if she denied him now he would not try to force or coerce her; they had gone far beyond that, and she sensed that he was as taken off guard as she was herself by their explosive response to one another.

This was the coming together they should have shared seven years ago, she thought intuitively; this was why she had never been free of him. Unconsciously she moved, reaching up towards him, the afternoon sun slanting in through the windows and outlining her breasts. There was a clear line where her tan ended and Slater traced it slowly, his dark gaze absorbing the reactions of her body, making her feel that in his mind already he possessed her and filled her.

Her fingers touched his waist, her hair golden against the dark fabric of his pants as she leaned forward and pressed tremulous lips to the firm skin just above his belt.

'Chrissie . . .' His response was explosive, his head lowering until his mouth touched her nipple. Fierce, almost unbearable pangs of pleasure shot through her at his touch, her teeth unwittingly nipping erotically at his skin, her body clenching beneath waves of fiery pleasure as without any gentle preliminaries Slater's tongue rasped the sensitive peak of her breast, his mouth tugging compulsively, while his hand struggled to release the fastening of his pants, his urgent movements inciting Chris to help him, and to shiver in primaeval female responsiveness at the sight of his naked, aroused body.

She wanted to touch him; a desire increased by his fierce possession of her breast, but trembled on the brink of doing so, until he released her tender nipple to mutter a plea against her skin that made her go hot with reaction and response.

As though to underline what he had said, his mouth moved downwards over her body, his tongue circling the smooth indentation in her belly, his fingers deftly untying the strings of her bikini bottom.

Just for a second Chris felt acutely self-conscious. She raised her head, intending to murmur an instinctive protest, but the words died unsaid as Slater looked directly at her, and she trembled beneath the fierce need burning in his eyes.

'You're so very, very beautiful . . .' He said the words slowly, as though barely aware of having spoken them, his hand pushing away the fabric of her bikini. Just for a second it rested against her body, and Chris was stunned by her muscles' instinctive response; by the tightly coiling sensation building up inside her that made her ache to arch against the hard pressure of his hand, to . . . She closed her eyes, shivering with the shock of her own sensuality.

'Chrissie . . .' She felt a touch as light as butterfly wings against her thigh, and then gasped at the intrusive stroke of Slater's fingers, half shocked half thrilled by his intimacy. It was almost as though he had read her thoughts; had known ... She opened her eyes to speak to him and was transfixed by the sight of his dark head leaning against her thighs. The gold eyes would not allow hers to slide away, hot colour mounting her skin as he deliberately placed his mouth against her skin. Hot shivers of pleasure surged through her. Her body seemed to melt, opening to him and she gasped, shuddering beneath the caressing intimacy of his fingers.

'Touch me, Chrissie,' he commanded in a hoarse voice. 'Touch me ... kiss me, the way I'm touching and kissing you ...'

Almost like an automaton she obeyed him, tensely at first, overwhelmed by the intimacy of what she was doing, but the heat of his skin, the sheer pleasure of hearing his raw sounds of desire, the responsiveness of his body to her lightest touch, soon obliterated every trace of shyness.

Her own body was equally responsive to him, arching wantonly to his lightest touch, her mind cast adrift by her body as she gave in to the mindless ecstasy his touch evoked.

His mouth against her thigh made her ache with hunger but when it moved higher she tensed instinctively, thrown into shivering uncertainty.

'Chrissie?' Slater's voice registered her unease, and suddenly fearing that he might withdraw from her, Chris said urgently, 'Slater ... please ... I want you. I ...' Tears spurted unexpectedly from her eyes, as he moved—away from her or so she thought, until she realised he had joined her on the cushions, his body hard and warm against her own as he took her in his arms, tracing the course of her tears with his tongue.

'I want you too.' His words were confirmed by the aroused weight of his body. Her fears subsiding Chris arched upward instinctively to meet it, gasping as the full intensity of her inner need washed over her, and she responded blindly to the urging of Slater's hands and body, revelling in the rhythmic thrust of his maleness against her, startled by her reaction to the sudden brief spasm of pain that for one second threatened to overcome pleasure. She felt Slater's fingers tighten and opened her eyes to find him looking disbelievingly back at her. She had forgotten that he hadn't known she was still a virgin. She thought he was going to speak, to withdraw from her, and pressed herself fiercely against him, holding him to her, kissing him passionately, her teeth catching on his lower lip as she felt his response in the powerful surge of his body into hers.

She knew she cried out—in pleasure not pain, but the sound was swallowed by Slater's mouth, fiercely enmeshed with hers, schooling the fierce tide of need swelling through her just as his body controlled her untutored physical response, nurturing it until she thought she would simply explode, dissolve, with the intensity of it. The power of the spasms of pleasure wracking her made her cry out his name, conscious briefly of his own harsh exclamation of pleasure, and filled with an intensely female sense of accomplishment that she had satisfied him. Even as she tried to register the thought the world started to whirl in a blur round her. She was going to faint Chris realised in stunned disbelief. . . . Slater had just made love to

her and she was going to faint. Darkness welled up
and claimed her, spinning her dizzily round. She
was aware of Slater calling her name, but she
could not summon the energy to respond.

Her faint could surely have lasted only seconds,
Chris thought muzzily, opening her eyes, blushing
furiously as she discovered that Slater was bending
over her, once more fully dressed.

'Chris . . .' His voice was harsh, the expression
in his eyes so cold that she shivered beneath it. He
had covered her with her wrap, she realised,
suddenly glad of its brief protection. 'Chris . . . we
have to talk . . .'

No words of love or praise, she realised bitterly,
but then what had she expected?

'No . . . No . . .' Panic edged up under her voice
and she struggled to conceal it, sitting up and
clumsily pulling on her robe. When Slater moved
to help her she flinched away from him as though
the contact burned. He dropped her arm immediately, backing away, his mouth tense.
'Chris . . .'

'No . . . no, don't say anything, I don't want to
hear.' She stumbled to her feet, half stumbling and
half running to the door. She had forgotten it was
locked and banged on it impotently with her fists,
tears streaming down her face. 'Let me out of
here,' she demanded half hysterically, not knowing
why she was crying or why she was filled with this
impulse to flee, knowing only that she had to get
away . . . that she had to escape Slater's presence.

'Chris . . .' He came towards her and she backed
away.

'I'm not going to touch you.' His voice was
terse, his back turned towards her as he unlocked

the door and opened it. She bolted through it like a terrified hare, not stopping until she was safely inside her own room. What had caused her flight she didn't know. Now that her sexual hunger was appeased she felt bitter and ashamed. She loved Slater, but he did not love her, and worse still he now knew how she felt—he *must* do—he *must* recognise the reason why she had retained her virginity for so long—and the reason she had been so impatient today to lose it. Shame scorched her skin. If only she could simply disappear she thought helplessly. If only she never had to face him again, but there was Sophie to consider. She simply could not walk out on the little girl now. Surely *her* future; *her* good health was more important than selfish pride? Natalie might not have made her Sophie's guardian for any love of either of them, but she was going to do all she could to carry out her task properly. Somehow she would just have to face Slater and endure his mockery. Somehow ... but please God not just yet, she thought achingly as she curled up on her bed. She couldn't face him just yet.

CHAPTER SEVEN

SHADOWS were lengthening in the garden when she woke up. Downstairs a door slammed and her body tensed, her eyes fixed on her closed door, in mute dread. When Slater came in she shrank back under the bedclothes.

'Chris.' His voice was sharp. 'Sophie seems to be missing.' The very real anxiety she could detect in his eyes banished any suspicions she might have had that he was making it up.

'Mrs Lancaster gave her tea as usual and she went upstairs to read. When she went to get her ready for bed she couldn't find her.'

'I'll help you look.'

She pushed back the bedclothes, avoiding meeting his eyes as she swung her feet to the floor.

'I've searched the house and garden already. Now I'll have to ring the police.' He was out of the door before she had left her bed. She had dreaded coming face to face with him again but now their mutual concern for Sophie over-rode any embarrassment Chris might have felt.

Dressed and downstairs she was just in time to catch the tail end of his telephone conversation.

'Yes I understand how you feel, Sarah,' she heard him saying, 'but obviously I can't take you out to dinner tonight ... Yes ... yes ...' He sounded tersely angry and Chris wondered at the other woman's lack of concern for Sophie. After all she was Slater's child and she thought Sarah would have cared about her for his sake if not for the little girl's own.

Anxious for something to occupy herself with, Chris went out into the garden. It was very large and parts of it were almost overgrown. Sophie could easily be lost in it, but Slater had said he had searched it and knowing him as she did she owned that that search would have been a thorough one.

She wandered down the drive and out on to the road. It made her blood run ice in her veins to contemplate the fates that might have befallen the little girl. She frowned remembering how distressed she had been by John Howard's visit. She hadn't even had time to tell Slater about her humming, Chris reflected retracing her steps back to the house. She found Slater in the study, his back was towards her. He was studying a framed photograph he held in his hands. Chris didn't need to see it to recognise the photograph of her cousin and Sophie which normally stood on his desk. Inwardly she wept bitter tears of pain, but outside she strived to appear calm as she approached the desk.

The naked ache of agony she had discerned in Slater's expression was wiped clean as he saw her, the photograph restored to its rightful place.

'It might not be important,' she began tersely, 'but Sophie seemed very upset this morning while John was here. He explained to me . . .'

'He did, did he?' Slater laughed with harsh bitterness. 'The Chris I remember wouldn't have . . . Oh for God's sake what's the use . . . Yes, it *is* important,' he went on bitterly. 'Surely even *you* can recognise that much . . . Dear God when I think of what could happen to her . . .' His voice was suspended and Chris wondered on a shock wave of horror if he blamed her for Sophie's disappearance. His next words seemed to confirm her fears. 'Sarah warned me against letting you stay,' he ground out savagely, 'and I'm beginning to think she might be right . . .' He strode past her without another word leaving Chris to stare painfully after him.

Could Sophie have run away because of John's visit? Had she perhaps feared that they might be a forerunner to more tests? More visits to hospital which Mrs Lancaster had already told Chris she hated? But where would she go? Unbidden the memory of her book in Sophie's hands tormented her. The cottage! But surely Sophie could not have gone there? A two mile walk or more and all on her own. Someone must surely have spotted her.

No, she was being ridiculous to even think of such a thing as Slater would no doubt tell her were she foolish enough to confide her thoughts to him. But what if she were right . . . what if Sophie had . . . There was only one way to find out, Chris thought numbly heading for the front door and picking up her keys on the way.

Ten minutes later she was pointing the car down the lane that led to the cottage. Already it was dark enough for her to need headlights and the thought of Sophie walking all alone down this narrow, overgrown lane made her ache with fear for the little girl.

The cottage was all in darkness. Getting out of the car Chris berated herself for her stupidity. She was just wasting valuable time which would have been far better expended in searching closer to home. Sophie could not possibly be here.

The cottage door wasn't locked. Chris remembered that she had not locked it after her last visit anticipating the arrival of the workmen who were to give her the various estimates she wanted.

The door creaked slightly and swung inwards. The sound of tiny scampering feet brought the fine hairs on Chris's skin bolt upright. Mice ... Shuddering she found the light switch.

The room looked no different than it had on her last visit. 'Sophie . . .' she called the little girl's name softly, feeling foolish. Of course she was not here . . . A quick inspection of the kitchen and dining room confirmed this view. Only upstairs to check now, Chris throught wearily already regretting her impulsive action in coming here. The stairs creaked as she climbed them, reminding her of how precarious they were. She hadn't bothered with the light and she cursed softly as one stair gave way beneath her foot. The wood felt soft and rotten and she grimaced anticipating the cost of replacing it. The whole place was probably riddled with damp.

At the top of the stairs she called Sophie's name again. Silence . . . Her ears stretched to catch the slightest sound registered a faint . . . what? Shivering faintly Chris hurried into her old room, stopping dead when she saw the small, huddled up figure on her old bed.

'Sophie . . .' Her relief turned to fear as she reached the bed and discovered how cold the little girl was, her eyes glazed and unseeing as they stared right past her. 'Sophie, it's me. Chris . . .'

she said softly, fear touching ice fingers at her
heart. What had happened to Sophie to cause this?
'I'm going to take you home to Daddy,' she said
quietly. 'Come on now . . .' Sophie's small body
was rigid and tense, so much so that Chris feared
to move her. Her eyes, normally alight with
warmth were empty, vacant almost, and that more
than anything frightened Chris. What should she
do? She daredn't risk moving Sophie by force in
case her reactions drove her even further into her
trauma, and yet she dreaded leaving her here
alone . . . If only the cottage had a 'phone . . .
There was one at the bottom of the lane, and the
lane led only to the cottage. It would take only
minutes for her to get there . . . minutes in which
Sophie would surely be safe? As these thoughts
raced through her mind Chris tried to appear
outwardly calm.

'We've been worried about you,' she told the
little girl, hoping to see some glimmer of response
in her empty eyes, praying that she could make
Sophie respond to her; that she needn't leave her
here, but could take her with her back to Slater . . .
If only she had told him her suspicions; if only she
had not feared his rejection and mockery more
than she had trusted her own instincts. It was
useless to think of 'if onlys' now she told herself.
'Please look at me Sophie,' she begged. 'Let me
take you home to Daddy.'

'I don't have a daddy . . . *she* told me I
didn't . . .' The sound of her hoarse, rusty little
voice transfixed Chris almost more than the words
she was uttering, and then it hit her, Sophie had
actually spoken. 'Sophie . . . Sophie darling . . .'
She rushed over to the bed, hugging her,

murmuring foolish words of praise, soaking her fair hair with her tears, but Sophie was completely unresponsive. So much so that her elation died. What on earth could Sophie mean? She didn't have a daddy? Slater thought the world of her; he was so gentle and caring with her that often she found herself envying her. Just this evening studying her photograph there had been such pain in his eyes that Chris had ached to have the power to soothe it.

'Sophie, listen to me,' she exhorted softly. 'You do have a daddy and Daddy loves you very much. I know he does . . .' There was absolutely no response. She had come out dressed in jeans and a thin tee-shirt and now Chris shivered. The cottage was both cold and damp, the musty scent pervading everywhere creeping into her lungs. What on earth ought she to do? Sophie's almost trance-like state decided her. She daredn't risk moving her forcibly; specially not in view of her extremely disturbed state; she would have to drive down to the end of the lane and ring Slater.

'Sophie, I'm going to go out now and telephone your daddy . . .' It seemed pointless talking to her, but she couldn't simply leave without an explanation Chris thought numbly and who knew perhaps if she talked she might get some response. 'I won't be long,' she promised opening the bedroom door. 'You wait here for me. I'll be back just as soon as I can.

Her heart thumping painfully she hurried downstairs, in her haste and anxiety forgetting the rotten step. As her foot went down into nothing she cried out and pitched forward into endless darkness, pain exploding inside her skull.

Where on earth was she Chris wondered muzzily opening her eyes. For a second she thought she was still in the summerhouse ... but no it was far too cold and there was no sunshine. Heat ran through her body as it remembered Slater's lovemaking. She moved her head restlessly trying to escape the memories, crying out as pain lanced through her temple. She put her hand up to it instinctively, wincing as she felt the warm stickiness there. Now she remembered. She had missed her step and fallen down stairs in the cottage. Sophie ... Fresh panic surged through her as she remembered the little girl ... At least Sophie could not have left, she reflected glancing at the stairs; half of them had given way as she fell and there was now a gaping hole where the staircase had been. The downstairs lights were on; they might alert someone to their presence.

She must try to get to the 'phone. She tried to get up and bit back a fresh gasp of pain as her ankle buckled underneath her refusing to take her weight. Had she broken it? Chris wasn't sure, but she did have to admit after two more attempts to stand on it that she wasn't going to be able to get out to the car. That meant that she and Sophie were trapped here until someone found them. Thank goodness she had put the downstairs lights on. Someone might see them and be alerted to their plight. It was a faint hope she recognised. No one used the lane and there were no other houses nearby.

Would Slater eventually decide to come and

investigate? Grim pictures of herself and Sophie starving to death flooded her mind, firmly rebutted by her common-sense. She was being ridiculous. The most they would have to wait was probably until tomorrow morning when surely one or other of the workmen would be along to survey the cottage. It was scarcely a comforting thought. The night stretched out ahead of them, long and very, very lonely. Sophie! Chris's heart lurched in panic. 'Sophie . . .' she called softly . . . 'Sophie . . . it's Chris. Can you hear me?' There was no response. She tried again several times, dragging her throbbing ankle behind her as she moved closer to the stairs.

The pain moving engendered made her head swim. She had barely eaten all day and now the traumas she had endured were beginning to take their toll. Her head throbbed muzzily, and the room went black whirling sickeningly round her. How many times in the hours that followed she slipped in and out of consciousness Chris did not know. She must be suffering from concussion she reflected at one point, trying to sort out her muddled thoughts; thoughts threaded through with tormenting images of Slater. It was just as well she thought unhappily at one point, that Sophie was unaware of their situation. At least the little girl was saved the terror that stalked her. How did *she* know what fears tormented Sophie's young mind, she asked herself achingly. Why had Sophie made that comment about Slater? What was she doing at the cottage? Was it as Chris had once sensed, a place of a refuge for her? Her muddled thoughts ran into one another, pain making her long to give way to tears. Her body felt as though it had been beaten. Her back must have caught on one of the stairs as she fell, it ached so much.

'Sophie . . .' she called weakly, knowing there would be no response. 'Sophie . . .'

She must have slept because the next thing she knew it was light. Her body ached all over and she was shivering. Exposure, she calculated, almost as though she were an onlooker on her own pain. She looked down at her ankle. It was very badly swollen and bruised black and blue. She couldn't bear to move it. Her head throbbed and her eyes felt gritty.

'Sophie . . .' Her voice sounded thin and reedy, but her physical discomfort was forgotten as Sophie suddenly appeared at the top of the stairs, looking untidy and grave. But this time there *was* recognition in her eyes—recognition and concern.

'It's all right, Sophie . . .' she said weakly. 'I fell down the stairs. Don't come too near the edge, they're very rotten. Have you been asleep?'

The fair head nodded. No sign of any attempt to speak Chris noticed . . . Did that mean that Sophie wasn't aware of what had happened last night? It was so frustrating not being able to ask her.

'Did you come here to get another book?' she asked lightly, watching Sophie's small face. For a moment it crumpled and looked puzzled and then Sophie nodded, running back to the bedroom and then reappearing with an old Enid Blyton book.

'Good girl. You sit there and read it,' Chris encouraged. 'Some men will be here soon and

they'll take us home to . . . to your daddy.' Praying
that what she was saying was true, Chris watched
Sophie's face closely, but her only response to her
comment was a brief smile. She was exhibiting
none of the emotion she had shown last night
when Chris mentioned Slater. She glanced at her
watch. Seven . . . How much longer would they be
trapped here? If the stairs hadn't gone she could
perhaps have sent Sophie off with a message, but
then if they hadn't gone she wouldn't be lying here
unable to move.

Time crawled by. Chris tried moving and
groaned as pain shot through her body, willing it
away as she saw Sophie's worried expression. She
must not frighten the little girl . . . 'Throw me
down a book Sophie and I'll read to you,' she
offered, letting out a painful breath as Sophie
trotted off into the bedroom.

The book she dropped carefully within Chris's
reach was another Enid Blyton. Painfully turning
the pages Chris started to read. At times the pain
from her bruised body almost suspended her voice.
She was shivering badly and her head ached, fine
points of light dancing against her eyeballs making
her long to close her eyes and give way to oblivion.
When she eventually heard a car coming down the
lane, she almost didn't believe it . . .

'Sophie, run to the window and wave,' she
commanded tensely . . . It was hardly likely that
whoever it was wouldn't stop. The lane led
nowhere else, but she couldn't relax until she heard
slamming doors and male voices.

'Whose car is that outside?' she heard someone
ask as the door was thrust open. Two stunned male
faces looked down at her . . . Trying to smile Chris

focused blindly on their faces, and said foolishly,
'Thank goodness you're here . . .'

'Get on the 'phone to Doc Stafford,' she heard
the older man saying tersely. 'We'd best not move
her. Come a real cropper she has . . .'

'Please . . .' Chris fought encroaching unconsci-
ousness to tug on the man's sleeve. 'Please . . .
there's Sophie . . .' she managed to whisper . . .
'Upstairs . . .'

'Sophie? Isn't that Slater James's kid? The one
that's gone missing?' The sharp query was the last
thing Chris heard properly as blackness washed
down over her. Vaguely she was aware of comings
and goings, of voices, Slater's among them but
when she tried to reach out to them she couldn't
speak. Someone was lifting her . . .

'Slater . . .' she tried to get her tongue round his
name, but it felt numb and swollen.

'She's okay, I've given her a pain-killing
shot . . .'

'Okay?' Was that really Slater's voice, sounding
so rawly bitter. 'Concussion . . . a swollen ankle
. . . God knows how many bruises and contusions
. . . exhaustion and exposure and you say she's
okay . . .'

She barely had time to absorb Slater's concern
before the other voice spoke again. 'None of them
things that won't mend . . . and at least Sophie's
safe . . . Wonder what made her come down here
. . . You'll have to ask your friend when she's
recovered. Obviously she must have suspected . . .'

'Then why the hell didn't she tell me instead of
coming down here alone?'

The savagery in Slater's voice pierced through
her. No doubt he blamed her for the delay in

finding Sophie. She started to cry slowly, consciousness receding.

'Chris ... Chris ...' She knew it was Slater calling to her but she couldn't respond. She dared not for fear of what her response would reveal. It was easier by far to simply slide down into the welcoming blackness that reached out its arms to embrace her; arms far safer than Slater's had ever been.

CHAPTER EIGHT

IT was several days before her doctor pronounced Chris well enough to leave hospital. Although her actual physical injuries had been relatively slight he had been concerned that she might be suffering from concussion. To tell the truth Chris found the events of the evening of her accident very blurred and shadowy. All that she could remember properly was hearing Sophie speak; the little girl's anguished words were carved into her heart, but she was reluctant to mention them to anyone. Although kind and concerned the hospital staff were so brisk that she feared they would believe she was imagining things and perhaps even keep her in hospital for further tests. She was far too thin Dr Stafford complained, and Chris was forced to admit that she had lost weight since coming to England.

Mrs Lancaster had been in to see her, and from her Chris had learned that Sophie had suffered nothing more than a cold after her ordeal. 'You know what kids are,' she said cheerfully, 'although we still haven't been able to find out why she went there in the first place.'

Chris herself wasn't sure, but she did know that something that had happened that afternoon had triggered off Sophie's flight, and that something it seemed was somehow connected with John.

Slater came to pick her up. She had wanted to refuse to go with him, but could see no way of doing so without causing a scene. He walked into the ward, tall and virilely healthy-looking in jeans and a thin cotton shirt. Chris could feel her body pulsing in silent response to his presence, and she averted her head unable to bear the pain of looking at him without betraying how she felt.

'Chris . . .' He hadn't been to see her during her stay in hospital, but then why should he? She meant nothing to him. She bit her lip remembering the heat of his body against hers in the summerhouse and amended her thoughts. He had wanted her physically, he had told her that much but there was no desire now in the golden eyes as they slowly searched her pale face. 'How are you feeling?'

'I'm fine . . .' A cowardly impulse made her add huskily, 'I really must think about leaving soon . . . Sarah was right, I don't seem to be helping Sophie.'

She turned away from him not wanting him to see the defeat in her eyes. She had come to Little Martin so buoyed up with hopes and ideals, but now they were all gone. The indifference to Slater she had been so proud of had been nothing more than a mental sham erected by her mind to protect her vulnerable heart—now it had been destroyed. Far from helping Sophie, all she seemed to have done was to precipitate another trauma. Had she been pushing the little girl too hard, demanding too much of her? When Slater didn't speak she continued slowly. 'I feel responsible for her disappearance . . . It must have been because of something I said or did . . .'

'Not necessarily.' His cool denial made Chris turn her head and look up at him in surprise.

Slater too had lost weight, she recognised numbly. His face was thinner, revealing hard bones, but then he must have endured agony wondering what had happened to Sophie.

'Why did you invite John Howard to the house?'

Chris closed her eyes on a wave of pain. They'd only been together for five minutes and already he was back to accusing her; condemning her. 'Not because I wanted him to make love to me,' she assured him bitterly. 'No matter what you might think of my morals or lack of them . . .' She broke off colouring hotly and shivering.

'That's another subject we have to discuss,' Slater told her curtly. 'I *am* aware that I seem to have been guilty of some error of judgment Chris, but now is neither the time nor the place.'

Of course it was only natural that he should be more concerned about Sophie than he was about midjuging her, Chris told herself firmly, and yet there was pain in acceptance of the knowledge and with it came the death of her faint, only just now admitted, hope that somehow the fact that she had had no lover but him would bring about a change of heart within him. What had she expected, she derided herself. A declaration of undying love?

'Well?' His curt tone reminded her that he was still waiting for an answer.

'If you really want to know why don't you ask John himself,' she demanded childishly, 'I'm sure you'd much rather believe him than me.'

'On this occasion I'm quite prepared to accept what you have to say.'

The faintly sardonic inflection to his voice made Chris look more closely at him, not sure if it was directed at her or at himself. The gold eyes were shuttered, unreadable, but there was tension in the way he held his body.

'It was because of Sophie,' Chris told him huskily. 'We were exercising together ... just a game really and then I heard her actually humming ... I didn't know what to do ... I was frightened of provoking the wrong response from her ... so I 'phoned John.'

'Humming?' The fierce glitter of hope burning his eyes to deep topaz made Chris's heart lurch in sympathy. Whatever else she could accuse Slater of, not loving his child was not among them. 'John said it was probably an automatic reaction,' she explained shakily. 'The tune was one that had been in the hit parade just before Natalie died. Sophie had probably heard it dozens of times,' she added, remembering her cousin's predilection for popular music. Natalie had never been able to endure silence or her own company; always she must have noise, activity ... Hers had in truth been a restless spirit.

'Why didn't you tell *me* this?' His fingers gripped her arm, darkly tanned against her paler skin. Chris flinched automatically instantly remembering the last occasion on which he had touched her, unaware of how huge her eyes looked in the hospital pallor of her face.

'It's all right, Chris.' Slater's voice was clipped and derisive as he removed his hand. 'I'm not about to force myself on you ...'

She flushed darkly, believing the comment to be a cruel taunt designed to remind her just how little force had been needed—none if she was honest, because she had wanted him with a need that probably over-rode his own. Her need, unlike his, had been fuelled by love.

'I wanted to tell you, but you were at work,' she reminded him, 'and you said you weren't coming back until late . . .' She frowned remembering his unexpected appearance. 'Why did you tell me that, Slater?' she asked him bitterly. 'Was it because you wanted to catch me out? To prove perhaps that I wasn't a fit person to be involved with Sophie? I might have guessed that you'd find some subtle way of getting rid of me . . . that always was your style wasn't it?'

'*My* style?' He gave a short bark of laughter. 'My God that's rich coming from you. Perhaps I came back because I couldn't endure being away from you any longer.'

He said it so derisively that for a moment she actually wanted to hit him, but she controlled the impulse saying quietly, 'Us quarrelling won't help Sophie, Slater.'

'No.' He frowned. 'I think I know what made Sophie disappear the way she did, but I can't work out why she should go to the cottage. To the best of my knowledge she didn't even know it existed. Natalie never visited her mother there after you left, and once the cottage was empty . . .'

'You're wrong, Slater,' Chris told him positively, 'Natalie had visited the cottage—and relatively recently. The first time I walked into it after my arrival I could smell her perfume—it was quite unmistakable, and Sophie must have been with her because she has some books of mine that can only have come from the cottage. Natalie would certainly never have thought to collect them and give them to her.'

'No, there never was any love lost between you was there?'

'I can't think why Natalie should go to the cottage,' Chris persisted. 'She always said she hated it when we lived there.' She glanced enquiringly at Slater, surprised to see how brooding and bitter his expression was.

'Can't you?' he said derisively. 'I should have thought it was obvious, although in view of recent discoveries perhaps I'm misjudging you again. I suspect Natalie used the cottage as a convenient place to meet her lovers,' he told Chris frankly.

She was stunned and completely lost for words, partly because of what Slater had suggested and partly due to his apparent lack of concern at Natalie's betrayal.

'You didn't care?' she whispered, only half aware that she was giving voice to her inner thoughts . . . 'You didn't . . .'

'Love her?' His mouth twisted. 'Natalie and I made a bargain, Chris, and whatever else was involved in it, love most certainly wasn't.'

It took her several seconds to grasp the truth. Slater had married Natalie because she carried his child. She ought to have felt pity for her cousin and one part of her did, but the greater feeling surging through her was one of relief. Slater had never loved Natalie . . . but he had *made* love to her, her brain cautioned, and at the same time as he was making love to you . . . he might not have loved Natalie, but he didn't love you either, Chris . . . It was undeniably true.

'Sophie seemed very distressed by John's presence.' Chris broke the heavy silence with the first thing she could think of.

'Yes . . . yes, she would be.' Slater's voice was clipped, his expression grim.

'What made you think of looking in the cottage, and why the hell didn't you tell me where you were going?' He asked the question just as the nurse came up to tell Chris that she was free to go.

'It was only a very faint hope—I felt silly telling anyone about it ... I didn't really believe it myself...

'And so instead you damned nearly killed ...' He broke off and turned his head away. He was furious with her, Chris acknowledged achingly and he had every right to be. She *had* jeopardised Sophie's life, but must he underline to her how very little *she* meant to him?

The nurse asked him to leave so that Chris could get dressed. He was waiting for her outside the ward, his expression still bleak.

'Are you sure you're okay?'

She must look an absolute wreck, Chris acknowledged painfully, or was it simply that Slater would prefer her to remain in hospital out of his way.

'I'm fine,' she told him tautly. 'Just as soon as I can make the arrangements I'll be leaving...'

'We'll talk about that later.' He was hustling her into his car. 'Dr Stafford wants to see you for a check-up in two weeks from now, so I shouldn't make any arrangements to leave before then if I were you.'

Chris gasped. 'He never said anything to me.'

'No?' Slater was plainly bored with the conversation. He leaned across her, deftly securing her seat belt.

'I'm not a child you know.' She knew she was being petty, but even the clinical brush of his fingers against her clothed body was a kind of agony she still felt too vulnerable to endure, conjuring up as it did images of other touches, far from clinical and burned into her memory for all time.

'And what about Sophie,' Slater demanded. 'What about all that pure motivating stuff you came out with not so long ago about having a duty towards her, or was that simply all a pose, Chris? A way of getting at me . . .'

'No! I love Sophie,' she told him shakily, 'but I don't think I'm helping her at all.'

'Same old Chris,' Slater taunted. 'You always did want instant results. Sophie needs time, Chris . . . time to adjust to Natalie's death . . . She loves you,' he told her unexpectedly. 'If you leave now it could do her irreparable harm.'

Why was he telling her this? Chris's head felt muzzy. He couldn't possibly want her to stay; he had already told her that; proved it to her . . . unless . . . she shivered suddenly despite the car's heating . . . Slater was an extremely sensual man . . . did he perhaps envision her as a willing bed-partner; someone he could use until such time as he tired of her?

'If I do stay, it will be strictly as Sophie's guardian.' The words were out before she could stop them, the sudden screech of car tyres as Slater pulled to an abrupt halt, shocking her. It was fortunate that they were on an empty country road Chris reflected numbly as his hands left the wheel and gripped her shoulders, the bitter fury in his eyes shocking her.

'And just what the hell does that mean?'

'Don't touch me.' She was in danger of total collapse, Chris thought weakly. If Slater didn't let go of her soon, she would be babbling her love to him, demanding far more from him than merely the angry grip of his fingers on her skin. 'Let me go. I can't bear you to touch me,' she lied huskily, desperate to put some distance between them. Slater's face looked grey, only his eyes alive as they burned into her. He released her slowly and sat back in his own seat.

'Don't worry, Chris,' he told her sardonically, 'I've far more important things to worry about than making love to you. You puzzle me you know, there's so much about you that's contradictory . . .'

'I'm a woman, Slater . . .' Somehow she managed to summon a small smile, 'It's an attribute of my sex . . .'

'I think I'm beginning to understand why you and Ray are still "friends". What happened, Chris? Did you hold out for marriage and he lose interest?'

Chris was totally nonplussed. 'I never wanted to marry Ray,' she told him in bewilderment.

'No . . . I forgot it was your career you wanted to further, wasn't it? And he was the vehicle you used to do it . . .'

Her heart was thumping erratically. 'Yes that's right.' For a moment she had almost forgotten the lie she had perpetrated all those years ago to save her pride, going to Slater and agreeing when he accused her of wanting to pursue a career as a model, even boasting a little of Ray's offer to help her. Anything to stop him from guessing how much his betrayal hurt her.

The rest of the journey was conducted in silence, Chris heaving a faint sigh of relief when they reached the house. Her ankle was still slightly painful, necessitating her taking care on stairs, but she was not prepared for Slater to pick her up in his arms when she hesitated at the bottom of them.

'Slater, put me down. I can manage . . .'

'Why bother, this way's much quicker.'

'I'm not an invalid you know,' she protested when he carried her into her bedroom and deposited her on the bed.'

'Perhaps not, but you have spent the last few days in hospital. Stafford said we were to make sure that you got some rest.' He was still bending over her and Chris had a suffocating desire to reach up and touch him . . . to feel his mouth against her own. . . . Perhaps something in her expression communicated her desires to him because she was conscious of a change in his expression, a darkening of his eyes that betrayed his purpose as his head came lower. 'Chris . . .' The way he said her name made her heart turn over; she yearned for him to hold her; to love her. His hand cupped her face, his thumb probing the softness of her mouth.

'Slater!' The sharply imperative sound of Sarah's voice forced Chris back to reality. She jerked away from Slater as though he was fire.

'I need to talk to you about Sophie. She's still extremely distressed.' She gave Chris a bitterly venomous look. 'You've brought her back then.'

No need to guess what Sarah thought about that. It was clear to hear in her voice. It was only when Slater left her room with the other woman that Chris remembered she had not told him about Sophie speaking. There would be other occasions, and anyway perhaps she would be wiser to discuss what had happened with John first. He was more likely to believe her than Slater who might even think that she was making it up, deliberately fabricating something to prove that her presence was of benefit to Sophie, lengthening her stay so that she could be near him. But Slater apparently wanted her to stay . . . Thoroughly muddled by her thoughts Chris closed her eyes and drifted into sleep.

It was Sophie who woke her. The little girl had crept into her room and was sitting on the end of the bed watching her. Chris gave her a warm smile, and said softly, 'Hello . . .'

The pleasure that shone in her brown eyes as Sophie returned her smile, made Chris's heart swell with love. 'Have you come to read to me?' she asked. Sophie had the inevitable book with her, she noticed, taking it when Sophie proffered it, guessing that she wanted her to read.

Half-an-hour later they were interrupted by Slater. 'So there you are. Sarah's been looking everywhere for you,' he chided Sophie gently. She pulled a slight face, but hopped off the bed in obedience to her father's instructions. Watching them leave, Chris frowned, remembering Sophie's anguished words. There had been no evidence today that she even remembered them, never mind doubted that Slater was her father.

She ate the lunch Mrs Lancaster prepared, dutifully, and was just wondering about getting up when Sarah marched into her room.

'I suppose you think you've been very clever,' she hissed without preamble. 'Making Slater feel so guilty that he has to keep you here, but it won't do you any good. Oh I'm not fooled even if he is.

You don't care about Sophie. It's all a pretext to stay here with Slater. He doesn't want you, you know,' she added viciously, 'any more than he wanted Natalie. He and I are going to be married.' She laughed mockingly when she saw the pain in Chris's eyes. 'Surely you guessed?'

'You're not wearing an engagement ring.' Chris knew that her voice trembled betrayingly.

'Not yet . . . we don't want to cause any gossip, besides it's the wedding ring that's the most important. Oh Slater may find you physically attractive,' she continued before Chris could speak, 'but he'd never let himself get involved with another member of Natalie's family. You're probably all tainted with the same brush . . . If she was mentally unstable, who's to say that you aren't too . . . Slater had enough of what that means being married to Natalie . . .'

'My cousin was not unstable,' Chris denied, knowing in her heart that she was lying . . . Had Slater complained to Sarah about Natalie's difficult temperament? She couldn't endure the knowledge that he must love the other woman. What would Sarah say if she revealed that only days ago Slater had made love to *her*? It was a hypothetical question because Chris knew she would not tell her. She had too much pride, and besides she knew that Sarah would put the same interpretation on his behaviour that she had herself. He had simply wanted her physically. Pain overwhelmed her.

'No?' Sarah's eyebrows arched contemptuously, 'Can you think of any other explanation for her . . . nymphomania . . .?' She laughed unkindly when Chris blanched. 'Oh come on, you must know what sort of woman she was. She couldn't leave any man alone ... I'm only surprised that Slater married her.'

'What would you have had him do?' Chris demanded bitterly, 'Ignore the fact that she was carrying his child?'

'*His* child?' Sarah's mouth twisted contemptuously. 'Slater didn't father Sophie. I doubt that even Natalie knew who did, but it certainly wasn't Slater. She told me herself that they had never once been lovers. Slater couldn't bear to touch her, you see.'

The shock of what she was saying stunned Chris. 'Not Slater's child? ... but ...'

'Why did he marry her? Natalie once told me they had some sort of pact. Slater doesn't talk about it.'

So there were *some* things that Slater didn't tell her, Chris thought numbly. 'I don't believe you,' she managed to get out finally, 'Natalie may have told you these things, but she ...'

'Was a congenital liar? Yes I know, but in this instance I believe her. She knew how Slater and I felt about one another ... She knew he wanted a divorce ... Why else do you think she took that overdose?'

It was horrible, far worse than Chris had imagined ... 'She was too selfish to let him go,' Sarah continued, angry spots of colour burning in her cheeks. 'She didn't want him for herself; she didn't love him but she wouldn't let him go ...'

'But Sophie ...' Chris protested weakly. 'He loves her ... she loves him ...'

Sarah shrugged. 'He feels a responsibility towards the child; he's that kind of man, but once we're married, there'll be no place here for Natalie's bastard. If you care so much about her, why don't you go back where you came from and take her with you . . . Neither of you are wanted round here,' she finished callously.

She was gone before Chris could react. She wanted to deny the truth of what Sarah had said, but some deeper instinct than logic warned her that it was true; that Sophie was not Slater's child . . . And Sophie knew it. Who had told her? Sarah? She was vindictive enough, Chris thought angrily. And what of Natalie? As though it had been yesterday Chris remembered her cousin telling her that she was carrying Slater's baby. After seeing the two of them together she had had no reason to disbelieve her, but according to Sarah they had never even been lovers. And if not Slater, then who . . . As though an inner door in her mind had unlocked, a picture flashed across her mind. Thrusting back the bedclothes, she walked unsteadily across to the dressing table, quickly extracting Ray's letter. Her fingers trembled as she picked up the photograph. The baby beamed back at her, the resemblance to Sophie so acute that she marvelled that she had not seen it before. She was standing ashen-faced studying the photograph when Slater walked in.

'Sophie's Ray's child.' She croaked the words, still only half able to believe them.

'He begot her, if that's what you mean,' came Slater's grim response. 'It isn't very pleasant discovering that someone you trusted has deceived you is it, Chris?'

'He can't have known,' Chris whispered positively, 'Natalie . . .'

'Natalie went to him and begged him to help her. He told her to go and get an abortion,' Slater told her curtly. 'She was on the verge of a breakdown when she came to me.'

'And you married her because . . .'

'My reasons for marrying her are nothing to do with you. If I were you it would be Ray I wanted to question—not me. What suddenly brought on this flash of insight, by the way?' he drawled tauntingly, and Chris had the nausea-inducing suspicion that he thought she had known all along about Sophie's parentage.

'Sophie spoke when we were at the cottage,' she said slowly. 'I told her I wanted to take her home to you, and she said to me, "he isn't my daddy . . ." '

'That bitch!' Slater's face had gone bone-white, his mouth hard and tense. 'Natalie must have told her. God knows she threatened to often enough, but I never thought . . .'

'It really doesn't matter what you thought.' How cool and controlled she sounded, Chris marvelled, watching Slater's face change, alert wariness creeping into his eyes as he watched her.

'All this proves is that Sophie is solely my responsibility. Just as soon as I can I'll make arrangements for both of us to leave . . .'

'You . . . now just one minute.' He almost snarled the words. 'Sophie stays right here with me . . .'

'Why?' Chris looked directly at him. 'You don't want her.'

For several tension filled seconds Slater merely stared at her with mingled loathing and contempt, and then at last in a clipped voice he said, 'You haven't changed have you, Chris? You always did have this facility for turning things round to suit your own convenience. Well not this time ... not this time.'

He slammed the door after him, leaving Chris to replace the photograph in its envelope. Even now she could barely take it all in, but she did know one thing. Ray would never have told Natalie to have an abortion. He was a deeply religious person; something that very few people knew. He himself had been illegitimate and often commented that had abortion been freely available in his mother's lifetime, he never would have been born at all. He had been abandoned as a baby and brought up by a succession of foster parents; and for that reason Chris could never see him refusing to acknowledge any child of his own. She *had* to speak to him, but the news that he had a six-year-old daughter was hardly something she could just announce over the telephone. And what about Sophie? Could the knowledge that Slater wasn't her father be the cause of her silence. She had to talk to John.

She wouldn't ask him to come to the house in case seeing him upset Sophie again, she decided. She thought for a few minutes. The cottage, they could meet there ... Once she had spoken to him she might be able to evolve some plan for Sophie's future. One thing she was sure of; she wasn't going to leave her here to be bullied and disliked by Sarah once she became Slater's wife. Slater had claimed that he wanted her. Why? Unless of course, it was simply that he wanted to prevent her from having the little girl? Could he really hate her so much? She was the one who ought to have hated him. She frowned. Why had he not *told* her why he was marrying Natalie ... why had he not explained? What did it matter now. Nothing was changed. He couldn't have loved her at all; it had been bad enough when she believed he had preferred her cousin to herself, but to know that he had married Natalie *without* loving her; to know that she had meant so little to him that he had so easily and carelessly dismissed her from his life, was bitter gall indeed.

CHAPTER NINE

CHRIS had to wait three days before an opportunity presented itself for her to ring John without being overheard by Slater. It was unsettling, knowing that he was in the house with her, and it made her stay in bed much longer than she had anticipated. On one or two occasions when he had come up to see her, she had the suspicion that that was exactly what he had wanted, and she couldn't help remembering his grim expression on the day they had left the hospital and she had announced her intention of getting back on her feet just as quickly as she could.

It was, she had told herself, just a matter of biding her time, and eventually she was proved right. On the third morning of her enforced stay in bed, Slater walked into her room and announced tersely that he was having to visit the factory.

'Don't even think of attempting to do anything foolish while I'm gone, Chris,' he warned her tersely, coming to stand beside her bed. He hadn't yet put on his jacket and the thin white silk of his shirt lovingly outlined the taut muscles of his chest. She ached to touch him Chris admitted to herself, half shocked by the intensity of her physical desire for him. Seven years ago, she had wanted him yes, but then she had been more than content to let him set the pace of their relationship and to follow his guidance whereas now . . . Now she was a woman, not an adolescent, she reminded herself wryly, dragging her eyes away from him, lest they betrayed something of her thoughts to him.

'We still have to talk.'

'No.' Her response was instantaneous and very revealing. She knew from his expression that Slater had heard the fear in her voice. His mouth had gone hard, his eyes almost amber as he stared down at her.

'Yes, damn you,' he contradicted thickly, adding, 'What are you so frightened of, Chris? Is it this?'

His mouth was on hers before she could move, his body blocking out the light, his hands imprisoning her shoulders against the mattress.

At first she twisted desperately from side to side trying to escape, but the fierce heat of his mouth; the need that his angry, almost bitter kiss aroused in spite of all her determination not to acknowledge it, overwhelmed her and her mouth softened beneath his, her arms going round his neck, stroking the softness of his hair.

She felt the bed depress under his weight and her treacherous body gloried in having him so close to her; offering no resistance at all when he slid aside one of the delicate straps of her nightdress to cup the rounded firmness of her breast.

The soft sound of pleasure she made in the back of her throat must have reached him. Chris felt him tense, registering her response. A bitter wave of shame flooded over her and she pulled away from him, turning her face into the pillow.

'Running away again, Chris?'

She felt his breath brush her skin, and shivered

involuntarily, trying to withstand the stroking probe of his thumb, as it moved over her lower lip.

'All right, I'll let you get away with it—this time. But you can't run for ever, Chris.' She felt him get up, her body instantly missing the heavy warmth of his, and as she heard him move towards the door she ached to call him back. Only after the door closed behind him was she able to expel a shaky breath. The sooner she left here the better, she told herself, listening for the sound of his car driving away. She didn't know what game he was playing with her, but what she did know was that if she allowed herself to be drawn into it, she would definitely be the loser.

Once she was sure that Slater was gone she dressed as quickly as she could, taking care not to put too much weight on her injured ankle.

Luckily Mrs Lancaster was out with Sophie, and there was nothing to stop Chris from ringing John.

Nothing apart from her conscience which urged her to tell Slater what had happened in the cottage, before she told anyone else. Why should she, she argued stubbornly with herself, Sophie wasn't even his child; he didn't really want her, he simply looked after her through habit ... And yet ... she had been so sure she had seen real love and caring in his eyes for the little girl.

John Howard was a doctor, she told herself. He would know far better than Slater what interpretation to put on Sophie's behaviour.

She got through to him straight away, and asked him if he was free for lunch. She didn't want him coming to the house again—not after what had happened last time.

He seemed rather restrained and cool towards her, but Chris urged him to accept. Perhaps he thought she was making a play for him, she thought bitterly. After all, if what Sarah had said about Natalie was common knowledge in the local's eyes, she might already be tarred with the same brush!

Eventually John gave way and agreed to meet her at the same restaurant where they had originally been introduced.

'I wouldn't ask, but it really is important,' she told him before ringing off, 'and I just don't know who else to turn to.'

She was in a fever of tension as she went back upstairs to collect her things, dreading Slater coming back and preventing her from going out. She daren't even leave a note for Mrs Lancaster just in case Slater came after her.

It wasn't until the taxi she had ordered to take her to the restaurant cleared Slater's drive that she was finally able to release her pent up breath. To her relief John was already sitting in the bar waiting for her. He greeted her briefly, looking tense and ill at ease.

'I'm afraid I don't have much time,' he apologised, ordering her a drink. 'I have a pretty heavy schedule today, and my wife wasn't too well this morning. I want to go home and check up on her before I go back to work.'

'I wouldn't have rung you if it hadn't been important,' Chris began defensively. 'I just didn't know who else to turn to ... It's about Sophie ...'

Quickly she outlined what had happened; when she had finished there was a long silence. John Howard's face was white, his eyes almost haunted. He looked so ill that Chris was shocked. She had never imagined him reacting so violently to her disclosures.

'Dear God, I've got to get out of here,' he told her unsteadily. 'Are you desperately hungry?'

Chris shook her head. Her stomach was churning it was true, but not through hunger. She had the sensation of being poised on an unexpected precipice, and it was an extremely unwelcome one.

'Did you drive here?' John asked tersely.

When Chris shook her head again, John took her arm and led her out of the bar. 'We'll go for a drive . . . Come on.'

He still looked ill when they were installed in the car, so much so that Chris felt extremely guilty.

'Look,' she began uncertainly, 'I'm sorry I bothered you with all this. I should have told Slater, but I was afraid he would dismiss it as sheer fantasy . . . That was before I learned that he isn't Sophie's father, of course.' She bit her lip wondering if she had revealed something that John didn't know, but his mind was obviously running on different lines from hers because all he said was, 'She promised me she wouldn't do it.' His voice sounded thick and strained, almost as though he found uttering the words a huge physical effort.

The road he took was a meandering country one that Chris dimly remembered. He pulled off it by a farm gate, and switched off his car engine. His face was still grey with pain, and Chris felt the nervous tremors of dread inside her building up as he finally turned towards her.

'God it's times like these that I wish I'd not given up smoking,' he said tensely. Abruptly he looked at her. 'You're sure that Sophie really spoke?'

'Quite sure,' Chris confirmed quietly, 'although she seems to remember nothing about it.'

'No ... no she wouldn't do ... it would be the trauma of being there in the cottage alone, especially after seeing me ... her mind would blot it all out I expect.' He took a deep breath and let it out on a shuddering sigh. 'None of us really knows what will happen about Sophie. A trauma as great as the one that originally caused her dumbness would be the ideal solution, but such things cannot be manufactured or controlled, and can go dangerously wrong ...'

'What was the trauma that originally caused the problem?' Chris asked quietly, 'No one seems to know ...'

'I know,' John told her, 'and so does Slater.' There was a long, long pause during which Chris held her breath wondering if he would go on and if he did, what he would tell her? Was Slater to blame for Sophie's illness? Was that what John was going to reveal to her?

'Is that why Slater feels so responsible for her?' she asked at last, needing to break the painful silence. 'Because he's to blame?'

'No ... no.' The anguished denial filled the interior of the car with emotion so intense that it was almost tangible. 'If anyone's to blame, it's me.'

The admission shocked her, robbing her of breath and the ability to rationalise. It took her several stupefied seconds to find the impetus to say huskily, 'You ... but how could that be possible?'

'Natalie and I were having an affair.'

Once again Chris was lost for words. Of all the men to be involved with her cousin, John Howard was the very last she would have thought of.

'But ...'

All that she was thinking must have shown on her face because John grimaced slightly and said, 'Yes, I know ... but there are times in our lives when we all do things we can't explain or analyse. Natalie was the very worst woman for me to become emotionally involved with. Demanding, petulant, selfish, greedy, unstable, she was all of those things—completely opposite from my wife, in fact, and perhaps that's where the attraction lay. It wasn't even a physical thing—at least not at first. She seemed so gay ... so pathetically lonely and vulnerable. She came to see me when I was doing some locum work for her regular doctor. She wanted me to prescribe tranquillisers for her. She couldn't sleep, she told me. She was thin, almost painfully so.

'I didn't realise then that her thinness was part of a deliberate campaign to get at Slater. I thought her husband the most selfish inconsiderate brute alive. She rang me up a week later. She needed someone to talk to she told me ... I fell for it ... It was very flattering to have such a beautiful woman wanting my company.

'We started meeting ... lunching together, and

then later going to the cottage. I'll never forget the first time we made love there. Natalie seemed to be on an intense high . . . She kept laughing, gloating almost . . . I knew there was something wrong, but I closed my eyes to it, by then I was too deeply involved. I refused to see what should have been obvious to me; that Natalie was desperately ill. We kept on seeing one another, and then one day she told me she wanted me to get a divorce. I told her it was impossible. She'd always known that . . . Whatever my feelings, I couldn't leave Helen.

'She seemed to change completely from the person I thought she was. She screamed and raved, calling me vile names, telling me she'd tell Helen about our affair. On and on it went until she'd exhausted herself. I admitted then that she was seriously mentally ill, but I couldn't break off our relationship—I daredn't. I tried to persuade her to go and see a specialist, but she had such severe hysterics that I tried to take the coward's way out then I'm afraid. I reminded her that she had a husband . . . a child . . .

'Her husband loved someone else, she told me and as for her child, Sophie! She hated Sophie she told me. She had always hated her. It was because of Sophie that she was trapped in her marriage with Slater. It was only later that she told me that Sophie wasn't even his child, by which time I was at my wits' end, desperate to prevent my wife from finding out about our affair, and terrified for Natalie who, it was becoming increasingly obvious, was very, very ill. I was caught in a cleft stick. In other circumstances I could have approached Slater and told him my fears, but because of my relationship with Natalie, that was impossible.

'She rang me up at home one evening demanding that I meet her at the cottage the next day. I went to bed that night determined to sort things out once and for all.

'She was jumpy and on edge when I got there. Slater was furious with her, she told me because she'd threatened to tell Sophie that he wasn't her father ... She was very wild and distraught. She wanted me to go away with her, to leave my wife. I explained that it was impossible. While we were arguing Sophie walked into the cottage. I didn't know it but Natalie had been taking her there. She had a thing about the place that I couldn't understand. She hated it, and yet she wanted to be there. Before I could stop her Natalie turned on the little girl screaming at her. She actually hit Sophie across the face before I could restrain her. Sophie was crying naturally. She wanted her daddy, she sobbed.'

He broke off, shuddering deeply, his eyes dark with pain, remembering what had happened, and Chris held her breath.

Her own chest felt tight and uncomfortable. If anyone else had told her this she doubted that she would have believed them.

'That was when Natalie told her that Slater wasn't her father ... I'll never forget it. Sophie just stared at her, and then she said slowly, "I hate you and I wish you'd go away and never, ever come back." She ran out of the cottage before I could stop her and when I started to go after her, Natalie held me back, screaming that she'd go straight to my wife, if I left her. I didn't know what to do. All my instincts, my training, urged me to go after Sophie, but my guilt, the knowledge of what Natalie could and would do to our life together, stopped me. And that's something I'll never cease to regret, never be able to square with my conscience—something I'll have to live with for the rest of my life.

'I never saw Natalie alive again after that night. I eventually managed to calm her down, and I took her home. Slater was away in London.

'He rang me the next day. I think I knew the moment I heard his voice. He asked me to go round. When I got there he told me that Natalie was dead. She'd taken a massive overdose cocktail of tranquillisers and God knows what. She left a letter, blaming me, saying that she was carrying my child, that I'd seduced and then abandoned her.

'I just didn't know what to say to Slater, but he made it easy for me. He knew what Natalie was like, he assured me. He also destroyed the letter. He told me that what had happened—the truth—would remain between the two of us. Natalie had been unwell and unbalanced for a while. Her own doctor could attest to that. He had in fact notified her own doctor the moment he discovered her. As you know they had separate rooms, and apparently it was Sophie who found her. Slater found her standing beside the bed, just staring at her mother. She hasn't spoken a word since.'

He laced his hands together and studied their blunt tips. 'It's quite obvious that Sophie blames herself for her mother's death. I never want to see you again, she said, and what happens ... her mother disappears. Of course we've tried to explain ... but she's a child ... and also deep inside her there's still hatred there for Natalie. Natalie never showed her any affection. In fact she seemed to hate her, but Slater . . .' He shook his head. 'Some days I wonder how I can live with the burden of guilt I have to carry. I look at my wife . . . I think of my life, and I wish to God I had the guts to tell her. She's strong enough to take it, much, much stronger than Natalie, much stronger than me, but I'm afraid that if I do tell her, she'll divorce me, and if Natalie taught me anything, it was just how much Helen means to me.'

It was all so very different from what she had imagined that Chris had difficulty in taking it all in. Far from being the cause of her cousin's death, Slater had in actual fact been more of a victim, both of her treachery and her unstable nature. In mentally depicting her cousin as desperately unhappy because of the unkind treatment of her husband, she had been about as far from the truth as it was possible to get. But that didn't alter her own vulnerability to Slater; nor the fact that she would be wise to get away from him before she revealed to him more than she wanted to know.

She was still as far away as ever from discovering why Slater had married Natalie in the first place—the only person who was ever likely to find out was Sarah, once they married. As his wife, she would have a right to know. And Sophie? What of her?

That Sarah didn't want Natalie's child to have a place in their lives Chris knew, but would Slater be in agreement to her having sole guardianship of the little girl? She had enough money now to retire from modelling; she could give Sophie a comfortable home, love, care; and perhaps even in time she might be able to introduce her to her real father . . .

But Slater *was* Sophie's real father, part of her insisted. Slater was the father she wanted; the father who had brought her up. How could Natalie have been so cruel? Instinctively she knew and she blanched at the knowledge, apart from Slater none of them were innocent of hurting Sophie. Natalie couldn't love her daughter because she looked too much like *her*, Chris acknowledged.

'Are you all right?'

She smiled painfully. 'I'm fine, just rather shell-shocked. No . . . please . . . You don't owe me any explanations or apologies . . . I'm glad you've told me though . . . It explains so much . . . why Sophie should be so upset after your visit.'

'Yes, poor child. Slater seems to think she believed that I might take you away from her as, in her eyes, at least, I had taken her mother.'

So Slater had talked to him about that. Chris chewed absently at her bottom lip. She needed time to think, time to sort herself out and come out with a concise, workable plan for her own and Sophie's futures—a plan that Slater would agree to.

'Shall I take you back now?'

They were only a couple of miles from Slater's house, as the crow flies, and Chris shook her head.

'No I think I'll walk back through the fields,' she told him. 'I need time to think—to re-assess things. The walk will help me.'

'Well take it easy on that ankle.'

As she got out of the car Chris turned to him. 'Thank you for telling me,' she said softly. It couldn't have been easy for him—she could see in his face that it hadn't. 'I think your wife is a very lucky lady,' she added encouragingly, 'and I think you should tell her—everything.'

'Perhaps I will. I want to, but finding the courage is another matter.'

Walking slowly back to the house, Chris tried to formulate some sort of plan to put to Slater. Should she simply confront him with her newfound knowledge and demand that he release Sophie into her care? After all there was no blood relationship between them. Or should she approach the matter more subtly; should she say that she knew that Sarah would not want the child once they were married?

And Sophie herself? What would she want? That she loved Slater Chris didn't for a moment doubt, but would that love be able to survive Sarah's hostility? Would she ever be able to regain her voice if she stayed with Slater? Wouldn't she have a far better chance of recovery in a completely new environment? She would have to take legal and medical advice Chris reflected—and she could be facing a hard and expensive battle, but she felt sure that she could give Sophie more than Slater and Sarah. What would happen when Sarah had a family? Sophie would be totally excluded, Sarah would make sure of that.

Wrestling with her thoughts she was half-way up the drive before she saw Slater's car. It was parked at an angle, tyre marks scored through the gravel as though he had stopped in a hurry. Her heart started to thud in panic. By now he must have discovered that she was missing. Why hadn't she thought about that? Because she had been too concerned with John's revelations and Sophie's future, that was why. He was back early. Had he returned especially to check up on her? Well she was a grown woman she reminded herself nervously, and if she wanted to go out for a walk then she was completely free to do so. Her ankle was virtually fully recovered; it barely ached at all. Slater was being ridiculous in refusing to let her go out.

As she rounded the corner of the house, hoping to walk in undiscovered via the drawing room french windows, she came to an abrupt halt, her pulses racing anxiously as she took in the small tableau on the lawn. Slater was crouching down on his heels, rocking Sophie's small frame in his arms. Mrs Lancaster stood worriedly by, and as she watched them, their voices reached her, Slater's terse as he demanded brusquely, 'When did you discover that she'd gone?'

'Just before lunch.' Mrs Lancaster sounded extremely upset. 'She'd just gone, no note ... nothing.'

'But all her clothes are still here ...'

Did they think she'd left permanently? Chris was horrified to discover what her innocently intended deception had led to. She took a step forward, kicking a small pebble as she did so.

The sound it made as it skittered across the crazy paved path seemed preternaturally loud in the tense silence that followed Slater's awareness of her presence. Across the half dozen or so yards that separated them their eyes met, Slater's topaz and darkly bitter, Chris's green and uncomfortably guilty. She waited for Slater to say something; to voice his smouldering rage, but it wasn't he who broke the thick silence, it was Sophie. Lifting her head she saw Chris, her eyes widening first in disbelief and then in tremulous joy. Racing towards her, she called her name, a thick, choked sound, but quite distinctly her name, Chris thought dazedly, going down on her knees and holding out her arms to catch her.

'Sophie ... Sophie ...' Tears stung her eyes, as she held Sophie slightly away from her. 'Surely you didn't think I'd really go just like that?' Watching the small delicate face, she remembered all that John had told her, and remorse flooded through her. Had Sophie thought that *she* had left her too?

'Sophie!'

Slater was standing beside them, one lean hand resting on Sophie's cheeks as he turned her face up towards his own.

'She said my name,' Chris said chokily.

'Yes, I heard her.' The quiet calm in Slater's voice warned Chris not to make too much of what had happened. 'And a rusty little squeak it was too ... It sounded more like a mouse with a sore throat than my Sophie.'

To Chris's great joy Sophie giggled. 'It wasn't a mouse, Daddy ... it was me.' Across her head their eyes met, and for once Chris wasn't ashamed of Slater seeing the emotion glittering there. His own eyes had darkened and looked over-bright.

'Take her inside,' he told Chris quietly, 'I'll go and ring the hospital. And Chris . . .' His mouth was grim as she turned towards him. 'Don't think this means that you and I won't be having that talk.'

CHAPTER TEN

OF course, it was hours before the excitement abated. Sophie, much to Chris's cowardly relief, insisted on sleeping with her and thus ensured that Slater would not be able to talk to her alone.

Once she realised what Sophie had thought, Chris was at great pains to assure the little girl that there had been no question of her leaving without telling her.

'I don't want you to leave here at all. I want you to stay for always,' Sophie protested.

They were alone in Chris's room. Downstairs Slater was no doubt making appointments for Sophie to see her specialists, Chris reflected, torn between giving the little girl the assurance she so badly needed and telling her the truth.

'I want you to be with me for always,' Sophie continued passionately.

This at least Chris knew she was able to respond to honestly. 'And I want to be with you, sweetheart,' she told her.

'Daddy said you must have gone back to America,' Sophie confided guilelessly. 'He said you had your career to think of.'

Chris's mouth tightened. She could just imagine how Slater had said that. 'There'll always be an important place for you in my life, Sophie.'

'Promise me you'll stay with me for always?'

At a loss to know how to respond, Chris was saved the necessity of doing so when Slater rapped briefly on the door and walked in.

'Bed for you, young lady,' he told Sophie, 'You've got a big day ahead of you tomorrow. We're going to see Dr Hartwell.'

Sophie pulled a face.

'He wants to hear this new voice of yours for himself. He didn't believe me when I said you sounded like a rusty mouse,' Slater teased.

Watching them like this it seemed impossible to believe that Sophie wasn't his child. He seemed to love her so much. To punish herself for her momentary weakness Chris interrupted coolly, 'Have you told Sarah the good news?'

'Not yet.' Slater's voice was blandly easy.

'I thought she'd be the first one you'd want to share it with.'

'I'll give her a ring later on . . .'

He seemed so casual, but then perhaps like her he realised that Sarah would not be particularly overjoyed by the news.

'Daddy, tell Chris we want her to stay with us for always,' Sophie interrupted. 'I want you to.'

'Oh, Chris is too big a girl to pay any attention to what I say,' Slater responded. 'She always goes her own way. I learned that a long time ago.'

Chris felt colour tinge her skin. Slater was obviously referring to the time she had told him that her career was more important to her than him; but then she had believed that he loved Natalie, and she had spoken those words to save her pride, knowing that she could not remain in Little Martin to watch as an onlooker his marriage to her cousin. Neither had she wanted him to guess why she was running away, so she had used the convenient excuse of her 'career'.

How angry he had been the first time she told
im that Ray had said she would make a good
model! Then she had barely paid any attention to
Ray's comment, simply shrugging it aside.
Modelling, or indeed any career, had been the last
thing on her mind; she had been dreaming of
marriage to Slater, bearing his children . . .

'Modelling? More like posing for girlie maga-
zines,' Slater had said scathingly, adding, 'Don't
you know how many silly little girls fall into that
trap every year? And once they're in it, no matter
how hard they fight they can't get out.'

Now she could see why he had doubted Ray's
sincerity, but then she had been puzzled by his
dislike of the other man.

And Slater had been wrong about him, of
course. Without Ray's help and encouragement
she would never have made it to the top.

'Are you happy now, Chris, now that you've
achieved your ambition?'

Happy? Unhappiness darkened her eyes
momentarily. Of course she wasn't happy in the
way that he meant; her career had been a way of
filling time, of silencing her thoughts, of keeping at
bay the knowledge that she still loved him.

'Of course.' How smoothly the lies slipped off
her tongue. 'I have a healthy bank balance, my
independence; some very good friends . . .'

'But no lover to share your bed at night,' Slater
taunted.

Sophie, Chris suddenly noticed, had dropped off
to sleep in his arms, obviously worn out by the
day. Her mind seemed to have gone blank,
refusing to provide her with a means of turning
aside Slater's question.

'Only because I don't choose to have one,' sh
managed at last.

'Why not, I wonder? It certainly isn't because o
any lack of physical desire.'

Her face stung with hot colour. 'Perhaps I
simply prefer my independence to being held in
thrall to some male.'

'But you can't deny that it is possible that you
could be "held in thrall", as you put it?'

The thrust was soft, but intensely painful.

Chris summoned all the skill she had learned in
her years of modelling, all her ability to assume an
expression at will.

'Possible,' she drawled smiling at him mockingly,
'but not probable.'

She held her breath waiting for him to react—to
retaliate, and expelled it in relief as she heard Mrs
Lancaster calling him.

'I'll take Sophie.' She held out her arms for the
sleeping child. As he passed her over, their hands
touched. Tiny electric frissons of awareness
shimmered over her skin. The moment he had
gone Chris hurried to the door and locked it,
thankful for the old-fashioned locks these doors
still possessed.

Just as soon as she could she was going to leave
Little Martin and take Sophie with her. Slater
would see the wisdom of such a course; he must
see it. Sarah would certainly agree with her, Chris
thought grimly.

It was comforting to wake up and feel Sophie's
small body curled into hers, although Chris felt
rather embarrassed when she had to pad across the
floor to unlock her door at Mrs Lancaster's
knock.

later said to let you both sleep in this
ing,' she announced carrying in a tray of tea.
s just gone down to the factory, but he'll be
ack soon. He's taking Sophie into Marton at
eleven, to the hospital there.'

While he was gone she would ring her agent,
Chris decided, she would know the best legal firm
for her to employ. Anxiously she bit her lip, would
Sophie turn against her for taking her away from
Slater? She hoped not.

The little girl was irrepressibly chatty over
breakfast, and when Chris helped Mrs Lancaster
to clear away the older woman laughed, 'I never
thought the day would come when I didn't want to
hear Sophie talking, but right now . . .'

'Umm, she seems to have got her voice back
with a vengeance,' Chris agreed. She put down the
plates she was carrying. 'I'm so sorry I gave you
all such a scare yesterday. I don't know why
Sophie should think I'd left. I'd simply gone out to
lunch with . . . with someone.'

'Oh, that's all right. Actually it was Slater who
decided that you'd gone for good. Fit to commit
murder, he looked when he came back and found
out you'd gone.' Her glance was speculative. 'If
Sophie hadn't been in the kitchen with me when he
came in saying that you'd upped and left, I doubt
it would ever have entered her mind. Of course she
was disappointed when we got back from the
shops and you weren't here . . .'

'I should have left a note,' Chris apologised.

'Well in view of what's happened, it's all worked
out for the best,' Mrs Lancaster said comfortably.

Chris made a point of staying out of the way
when Slater returned to collect Sophie. She very

much wanted to go with them, but Slater h
asked her to, and besides she wasn't sure if sh
up to the ordeal of his company.

Her attempts to get through to her agent we
frustrated by the lines being busy. She would just
have to wait until tomorrow Chris reflected when
she heard the sound of Slater's car returning later
in the afternoon.

She went downstairs to meet them. Sophie was
glowing with excitement. 'Dr Hartwell said I was a
miracle,' she told Chris proudly, 'and he said I
didn't sound like a rusty mouse at all.'

'He also said you had to rest,' Slater reminded
her wryly.

'I'll take her upstairs,' Chris offered. Looking at
him she had suddenly been struck by the lines of
pain and tiredness round his eyes. He had always
seemed so strong and invulnerable that she had
never noticed them before. She wanted to go up to
him and draw his head down on to her breast; to
comfort him. To combat this momentary weakness
she took hold of Sophie's hand and tugged her
inside.

Upstairs in her room Sophie was still arguing
that she wasn't tired, but within ten minutes of
Chris starting to read to her she was fast asleep.

It was a shock to find Slater standing just
inside the door, watching them. How long had
he been there? Her heart thumping unevenly,
Chris got up.

'You really care about her, don't you?' he said
quietly. 'How does it feel, Chris, to know what
you've given up?'

Reaction rioted inside her. Forcing it down she
said lightly. 'I'm only twenty-six, Slater. There's

still plenty of time for me to have a child, if I want one.'

'First you've got to find a man.' He said the words almost insultingly, and remembering what she had read of artificial insemination and the new scheme in operation in the States whereby a woman could elect to impregnate herself with the seed of some of the best brains in the world, she shrugged, 'Not necessarily, you . . .'

Almost at once his face darkened, his eyes smouldering dark gold. 'I what?' he snarled, totally misunderstanding her comment. 'I might have already have given you a child? If I have you won't get to keep it. No child of mine is going to be brought up by . . .'

'By what?' Chris shouted at him, nearly as furious as he was himself. 'By someone whose cousin is a nymphomaniac? What's wrong, Slater? Are you worried that I might have inherited the same tendencies as Natalie; that I might corrupt my own child?'

She was barely able to understand her own pain, knowing only that it had sprung from the bitter anger in Slater's eyes when he thought she might be referring to the fact that she could have conceived his child. Did he really dislike her so much? Belatedly she remembered Sophie. A quick glance at the little girl confirmed that she was still asleep. Brushing past Slater, she went on unsteady legs to her own room. Once there she sank down on to the bed, longing to give way to tears, but too wound up to do so.

When the door opened and Slater walked in she could hardly believe her eyes.

'Running away again, Chris,' he taunted. His

voice sounded odd, thick and husky, as though he was barely able to frame the words. 'Well this time there's nowhere to run to. Just answer me one thing honestly, have you ever regretted what you did? Have you ever wished for just one second that you hadn't put your precious career first? Why the hell did you come back, Chris?'

'You know why . . . I'm Sophie's guardian.'

'And that brought you back; a tenuous link with a child you'd never even seen? That's not the Chris I know. She never let emotional ties of any type mean anything to her.'

'That's not true!'

'Isn't it? Then how the hell do you explain the fact that you were able to walk out on me, without so much as a single word of regret?'

'All these years and you still resent that?' She could hardly believe it. She had never thought of him as being so egocentrical. He hadn't loved her; he had been planning to marry someone and yet after all this time he could display this almost excessive bitterness because she had left. 'I'm surprised you can still remember.'

'Oh I remember all right . . . just as I remember every hour of the nightmare my life's been since. Have you any idea what it was like married to Natalie wondering what the hell she was going to do next? When Sophie was six weeks old Natalie tried to smother her.' He watched her go white. 'Oh yes. She never loved Sophie; never wanted her. I had to watch her like a hawk, and then later there were men . . . Never one man for any length of time, until . . .'

'Until she met John,' Chris supplied for him. 'I met him for lunch yesterday. He told me all about it. I'm not Natalie, Slater,' she added quietly when she saw the thoughts reflected in his eyes. 'I thought when we were trapped in the cottage that Sophie spoke and I wanted to talk to him about it. He told me a lot more than I'd bargained on hearing.' She desperately wanted to ask him why he had ever married Natalie, but she didn't have the right. 'You might as well know,' she continued, 'that I want Sophie to come and live with me.'

The furious sound he made as he swore, silenced her. 'You bitch,' he exclaimed bitterly. 'You think you can take it all, don't you? Well you're not having Sophie.'

'She isn't your child,' Chris pointed out, 'and Sarah doesn't want her.'

'Sarah? What the hell's she got to do with all this?'

'Oh, come on, Slater.' She was getting angry herself now. 'Sarah told me you and she are getting married. She seemed to think that was why Natalie took her life—she said you'd asked her for a divorce. She doesn't like Sophie, you must know that. You'll have other children but Sophie is related to me by blood. I can give her so much, and I love her.'

'And you think I don't is that it? For six years she's been my child, and now suddenly I'm supposed to give her up? Well if you want Sophie, you're damned well going to have to pay for her,' he snarled suddenly, slamming the door closed behind him.

'How?' Chris was totally confused. What did he want? Money? Slater had always been relatively wealthy; money had never seemed to be a motivating force in his life. Her mind could not take in what he was saying.

'Like this.' He locked the door and came towards her, his intention written clearly in his eyes. Chris tensed and moved back; the eternal moves of prey and hunter. Deep down inside her tension began to coil in spirals of excitement. Slater wanted her; she knew it as instinctively and intensely as though he had said the word out loud to her. Her pulses thudded protestingly as he came closer, so close that she could see the yellow speckles in his irises.

'Slater . . .'

'Don't say anything,' he warned her thickly. 'You owe me this, Chris . . . this and all the thousands of other times you should have been in my arms and weren't. I don't understand it, damn you,' he muttered as he reached her and seized hold of her upper arms. 'You're not cold, or lacking in passion—just the opposite, and yet all these years there you've remained a virgin . . .'

Chris tried to summon a cool smile. 'Perhaps I just enjoy teasing,' she commented brightly, trying to shake free of his grip. 'I really don't think this is a good idea, Slater . . .'

'Really? Now I happen to disagree.' The silky softness of his voice shivered across her nerves.

'You're marrying Sarah,' Chris reminded him suddenly growing desperate.

'I'm not married to her yet. You owe me this, Chris . . .'

It was the second time he had voiced the emphatic claim. She didn't owe him anything, Chris thought bitterly; on the contrary, he was the one . . . Her thoughts became a confused jumble as his mouth touched hers, lingering sensually on the softness of her lower lip. Violence she could have resisted, but this tenderness, this feeling she had that he was willing her backwards in time were things she couldn't compete against. Her body wanted him; yearned for him far more hungrily now that it was aware of all that his possession could mean; than it had done in the old days, when his experience had protected her innocence.

The heat of his mouth as it moved on hers seduced her senses, her body burning where he touched it, stroking lightly over her clothes, until she ached to be rid of their constrictive layers and free to feel the oiled silk of his skin on her own. She felt him move slightly away and instinctively her mouth clung, her tongue tentatively begging him to stay.

'Chris!' The muffled sound of her name, almost tortured as he muttered it against her throat made her heart thud excitedly. She loved him so much she was willing to take even these crumbs, she acknowledged mentally. If Slater wanted to make love to her then she was more than willing for him to do so. In his arms she wanted to be for him all the woman he had ever hungered for; a woman he would remember all his life. She wanted their lovemaking to be something that marriage to Sarah would never be able to obliterate and if that was selfish then she was going to be selfish she decided, anguishedly.

'You don't know how much I want you.' The admission seemed to be wrung from him, his skin hot as he pressed his forehead against hers, his fingers tense on her body. The sudden sensation of power was so strong and overwhelming that she didn't even try to resist it.

'Show me.' She whispered the words against his mouth, teasing the taut shape of it with soft kisses, sliding her hands along his shoulders until her breasts were pressed flat against his chest.

The frenzied thud of his heart seemed to beat right through her, her insides curling pleasurably with excitement as his hands cupped her face, his mouth devouring hers, absorbing the taste and texture of it, as though it were some magical life force.

The heat of his palm against her breast melted her insides, her need finding some relief in the small sounds of pleasure she made deep in her throat.

'It's like listening to a kitten purring.' Slater mouthed the words against her throat feeling the reverberations of the small sounds increasing in volume as he unfastened her blouse and slid his hand inside.

Against the thin silk of her bra her nipples strained provocatively for his touch, her body arched along the length of his, supported by his arm at the back of her waist.

His mouth left her throat, and Chris opened her eyes reluctantly. Heat exploded inside her as she saw the naked desire glittering in his eyes as his gaze rested on the aroused thrust of her breasts.

'Kiss me.' The words seemed to come from a woman who was almost a stranger to her; a woman who seemed to know instinctively how to guide Slater's dark head to her breast; a woman who made no secret of the pleasure he gave her

when he pushed aside the fine silk and slid his
mouth over the hard nub of her nipple.

'Like this?' Slater's mouth caressed her other
breast, while Chris murmured her pleasure, her
hands clutching at the smooth flesh of his back.
Totally engrossed in the sharply erotic sensations
flooding her body as Slater's mouth suckled her
nipples, Chris was barely aware of him unzipping
her skirt until it slid free of her hips, and he lifted
her free of it, his hands sliding inside the barrier of
her briefs to hold her against him. His harsh groan
of pleasure at the intimate contact of their bodies
flooded her with love. Her fingers tugged at the
buttons of his shirt, her mouth fusing eagerly with
his, as her hips strained eagerly against him.

Beneath his shirt his chest was slightly moist, the
musky scent of his body enveloping her.

When he dropped down on one knee in front of
her to unfasten her stockings Chris quivered with
heady anticipation. For once in her life she wasn't
going to think or rationalise; she was simply going
to feel. But the fierce sheeting of pleasure racing
under her skin as Slater's mouth caressed the
tender inside of her thigh was something for which
she was totally unprepared. She pulled away
instinctively, trembling, caught up in coils of ever
tightening desire for him, a dark tide of colour
storming her skin.

'Chris . . . Chris . . . let me love you.' Slater's
skin was as flushed as her own, his voice thick,
barely recognisable.

Quivers of sensation arrowed through her like
darts of fire as he took her silence for consent and
his tongue wove delicate patterns against her
responsive skin, his hands deftly removing the silk

stockings. The dainty ribbon of her suspender belt slid to the floor the moment he unfastened it. Chris shivered as she felt the light brush of his fingers against the top of her thigh and then under the elastic of her tiny briefs. Dizzily she closed her eyes, wanting to touch him as he was touching her, aching for him to possess her body, to . . .

Idiotically, when he had removed her briefs she wanted to hide herself away from him, and as though he sensed the impulse he reached up, grasping her wrists, securing them lightly behind her body with one hand, while the other stroked slowly up the left hand side of her body, his fingers curling round her ankle, exploring the shape of her calf; her knee . . . Chris was shivering convulsively, long before she felt the gentle drift of his mouth along her inner thigh. His hand cupped her bottom, and she cried out aloud as she felt the intimate brush of his tongue against her body, wanting to pull away and yet too enfeebled by the tumultuous surge of pleasure rushing through her to do so.

The small sounds she had been suppressing clogged up her throat and were expelled in a tormented moan. 'Slater, please . . .' She wanted to make him stop what he was doing; to give voice to her shock at the intimacy of his caresses, but the fevered words of praise and encouragement he was groaning against her skin stopped her. She let him lift her on to the bed, holding out her arms eagerly to him as he removed the rest of his clothing. His body was perfect, she thought breathlessly studying it with open curiosity, unable to stop herself from touching, half in awe . . . half in love. A man's open physical arousal was something she had never witnessed before, and she was overcome by a feeling of pride that she should have such an effect on him, coupled with a need to show him how much his desire for her meant to her.

When she touched him hesitantly he tensed. Uncertainty flickered through her. In the old days although she had known that she aroused him, all the caresses between them had been initiated by Slater. She had never touched him intimately nor had he indicated that he wanted her to do so. Now she wanted to, for her own sake as much as his, but what if he didn't want her to?

She looked hesitantly up at him, and caught her breath. Desire burned fiercely in his eyes, every bone in his face sharp-etched; his body tensed. He swallowed and she watched the muscles in his throat move, like someone in a dream. Wanting him was the worst kind of agony; an ache that seemed to invade every muscle and cell of skin.

'Slater.' She murmured his name, her fingers stroking the firm sinewed surface of his thigh. Unlike her own it was covered in fine dark hairs. He didn't move, neither rejecting nor accepting her caress. She bent her head and touched her lips to his skin.

A thick inarticulate sound shattered the heavy silence surrounding them. Instantly Chris tensed and looked up at him, her heart thumping.

Need; hunger; anger; all were clearly discernible in his eyes. He closed them as she watched, sliding his hands into her hair.

'You make me ache so badly that I think I'm going mad with the agony of it. Don't play with me, Chris,' he warned her hoarsely. 'You're not nineteen now—you're old enough to know that I

want you in all the ways a man can want a
woman. I want to caress and arouse your body
until I can feel the pleasure flood through it. I
want you to touch and caress me in exactly the
same way, but not as some sort of experiment you
feel you have to embark on; not because it's a
reciprocal payment. Do you understand me?'

Of course she did. Her body ached in tune to his
harshly spoken words, feeling the pain; the
wanting that had given birth to them.

'I've dreamed of you for years,' she told him
slowly. 'Ached for you ... cried for you. I love
you, Slater,' she admitted huskily, bending her
head until her hair slid silkily against his thighs
and her lips caressed the hard maleness of him. His
fierce sounds of pleasure heated her blood, her
body pliant and eager for his, revelling in the
punitive, urgent rasp of his tongue and teeth
against the taut peaks of her breasts as he pulled
her away from his body and proceeded to make
love to her with an urgency that seemed to match
her own aching need for fulfilment.

The thrust of his body against and into her own
pierced her with waves of pleasure. Her mouth
clung feverishly to his, returning his drugging
kisses. Heat filled her and then exploded into
waves of pleasure. Beneath his mouth she called
his name. His mouth left hers, a harsh cry of
fulfilment echoing round the room as his body
found release. He kissed her again. Gently this
time, his lips pressing tender, almost adoring kisses
against her throat and breasts, his arms curving
her into his body.

Relaxed and drowsy, Chris was caught completely off guard when he said, 'Why did you say

you loved me? A slip of the tongue . . . Something you felt you ought to say, or was it simply the truth?'

Reaction rushed over her like a cold spring tide. She tried to move, but he wouldn't let her. Her humiliation was now complete, she derided herself. In her need for him, her love of him she had betrayed herself completely, while Slater had revealed . . . nothing.

She wanted to lie but she knew she couldn't. The words of an old saying came back to her. 'To thine own self be true.' Why should she demean herself in her own eyes by lying. What would it achieve now?

'Once long ago I lied to you to save my pride, Slater,' she told him quietly, 'I'm not prepared to do that a second time. Yes, I do love you.' She made herself look at him. 'I would think less of myself for making love with you not doing so, than I do for being foolish enough to do so.'

She was quite proud of her little speech but Slater didn't appear to have taken it all in. He was frowning. 'What do you mean you lied to me once?'

Mentally shrugging, Chris decided he might as well know the complete truth. Perhaps it would help dissolve his bitter distrust of her; help him to see that Sophie's place was with her.

'I'm talking about when I told you that my career came first. That wasn't the truth. I was desperately hopelessly in love with you, but Natalie had just told me that you were going to marry her, what was I supposed to do? I couldn't endure the pain of being rejected by you, so I went to Ray and told him I'd reconsidered his offer to help me become a model.'

'You believed Natalie, just like that?'

'Not just like that,' Chris admitted candidly. 'I saw her in your arms one day. I'd come here to see you. You were in the drawing room together . . .'

'That must have been the day she told me about the baby.'

'She told me she was carrying your child . . .'

Slater's mouth had thinned, his eyes dark with anger. 'She told *me* that you and Ray were lovers; that you'd told her you were tired of me, that you were going to leave Little Martin. She suggested we soothe each other's pride by marrying. I was half off my head with jealousy at the time . . . I couldn't bear to think that you didn't love me.'

Chris sat up, gathering the sheet round her. 'She lied to both of us,' she said slowly. 'Fooled us both . . . tricked us.' Unexpectedly tears started to well in her eyes and brim over on to her cheeks.

'Chris, please don't cry . . .' Slater's arms came round her, her head resting on his chest. 'It's over . . . the whole thing, and we're free to go on with our lives.'

What he meant that he was free of whatever he had felt for her—free to marry Sarah, Chris thought achingly.

'And you'll let me have Sophie?' She winced as he shook his head.

'Let you take away the only thing that's kept me sane these last six years? Do you know why I loved her so much initially, Chris? Well it was because she looked so much like you. I couldn't have you, but I could have a child who reminded me of you—who could have been *our* child.'

When she looked at him uncomprehendingly he added thickly. 'Chris, Chris, it isn't too late for us. I still love you . . . you love me . . .'

'You love me?' She said it wonderingly, despair giving way to joy.

'Of course I damn well do.' He tilted her face up to meet his own, kissing her with a depth of emotion that banished all her lingering doubts. 'Why do you imagine I was so anxious to get you back here; so disturbed to discover that you were still a virgin; so terrified that I might have hurt or frightened you that I daredn't come near you because I knew that if I did, I'd make love to you again . . . and again . . .'

'But Sarah,' Chris protested. 'She . . .'

'Sarah lied. I've never discussed marriage with her. I'd never marry her even if you didn't exist, simply because of the way she feels about Sophie.

'Chris, marry me just as soon as we can arrange it . . .'

'What and give up my successful career?'

She had only been teasing him, giving way to heady, drunken joy but the moment she saw the pain in his eyes she regretted the light words. 'Oh no Slater . . . don't look like that . . . I'd give up a thousand successful careers to be with you . . . Of course I'll marry you.'

'And Sophie?'

'She'll always be our eldest child. Perhaps one day we can tell her about Ray. I don't believe he can have known about Natalie. He would never have suggested an abortion. Perhaps she knew he wouldn't marry her and used that story to gain your sympathy. We'll never know.'

'Seven years of my life your cousin stole from

us. Seven years when we could have been together, when I could have woken up with you in my arms. Watched you bear our children . . . Seven years of loving to catch up on.'

'Then we'd better not waste time talking, had we?' Chris murmured archly. She stretched sensuously against him, delighting in his slow appraisal of her body, delighting in the freedom to show her love and know that it was reciprocated. 'I love you Slater,' she told him softly. 'I always have and I always will . . .'

'I sincerely hope so,' he told her thickly, 'because without you my life simply isn't worth living.'

Coming Next Month in Harlequin Presents!

839 BITTER ENCORE—Helen Bianchin
Nothing can erase the memory of their shared passion. But can an estranged couple reunite when his star status still leaves no room for her in his life—except in his bed?

840 FANTASY—Emma Darcy
On a secluded beach near Sydney, a model, disillusioned by her fiancé, finds love in the arms of a stranger. Or is it all a dream—this man, this fantasy?

841 RENT-A-BRIDE LTD—Emma Goldrick
Fearful of being forced to marry her aunt's stepson, an heiress confides in a fellow passenger on her flight from Denver—never thinking he'd pass himself off as her new husband!

842 WHO'S BEEN SLEEPING IN MY BED?—Charlotte Lamb
The good-looking playwright trying to win her affection at the family villa in France asks too many questions about her father's affairs. She's sure he's using her.

843 STOLEN SUMMER—Anne Mather
She's five years older, a friend of the family's. And he's engaged! How can she take seriously a young man's amorous advances? Then again, how can she not?

844 LIGHTNING STORM—Anne McAllister
A young widow returns to California and re-encounters the man who rejected her years before—a man after a good time with no commitments. Does lightning really strike twice?

845 IMPASSE—Margaret Pargeter
Unable to live as his mistress, a woman left the man she loves. Now he desires her more than ever—enough, at least, to ruin her engagement to another man!

846 FRANGIPANI—Anne Weale
Her sister's offer to find her a millionaire before they dock in Fiji is distressing. She isn't interested. But the captain of the ship finds that hard to believe....

Readers rave about Harlequin American Romance!

"...the best series of modern romances I have read...great, exciting, stupendous, wonderful."
—S.E.*, Coweta, Oklahoma

"...they are absolutely fantastic...going to be a smash hit and hard to keep on the bookshelves."
—P.D., Easton, Pennsylvania

"The American line is great. I've enjoyed every one I've read so far."
—W.M.K., Lansing, Illinois

"...the best stories I have read in a long time."
—R.H., Northport, New York

*Names available on request.

*You're invited to accept
4 books and a
surprise gift* Free!

Acceptance Card

Mail to: **Harlequin Reader Service®**

In the U.S.
2504 West Southern Ave.
Tempe, AZ 85282

In Canada
P.O. Box 2800, Postal Station A
5170 Yonge Street
Willowdale, Ontario M2N 6J3

YES! Please send me 4 free Harlequin American Romance®
novels and my free surprise gift. Then send me 4 brand new novels
as they come off the presses. Bill me at the low price of $2.25 each
—an 11% saving off the retail price. There are no shipping, handling
or other hidden costs. There is no minimum number of books I
must purchase. I can always return a shipment and cancel at any
time. Even if I never buy another book from Harlequin, the 4 free
novels and the surprise gift are mine to keep forever.

154 BPA-BPGE

Name   (PLEASE PRINT)

Address   Apt. No.

City   State/Prov.   Zip/Postal Code

This offer is limited to one order per household and not valid to present
subscribers. Price is subject to change.   ACAR-SUB-1

Just what the woman on the go needs!

BOOKMATE

The perfect "mate" for all Harlequin paperbacks!

Holds paperbacks open for hands-free reading!

- **• TRAVELING**
- **• VACATIONING**
- **• AT WORK • IN BED**
- **• COOKING • EATING**
- **• STUDYING**

Perfect size for all standard paperbacks, this wonderful invention makes reading a pure pleasure! Ingenious design holds paperback books OPEN and FLAT so even wind can't ruffle pages—leaves your hands free to do other things. Reinforced, wipe-clean vinyl-covered holder flexes to let you turn pages without undoing the strap...supports paperbacks so well, they have the strength of hardcovers!

Snaps closed for easy carrying.

Available now. Send your name, address, and zip or postal code, along with a check or money order for just $4.99 + .75¢ for postage & handling (for a total of $5.74) payable to Harlequin Reader Service to:

Harlequin Reader Service

In the U.S.A.
2504 West Southern Ave.
Tempe, AZ 85282

In Canada
P.O. Box 2800, Postal Station A
5170 Yonge Street,
Willowdale, Ont. M2N 5T5

MATE-1R

Take 4 books & a surprise gift FREE

SPECIAL LIMITED-TIME OFFER

Mail to   **Harlequin Reader Service®**

In the U.S.
2504 West Southern Ave.
Tempe, AZ 85282

In Canada
P.O. Box 2800, Station "A"
5170 Yonge Street
Willowdale, Ontario M2N 6J3

YES! Please send me 4 free Harlequin Presents® novels and my free surprise gift. Then send me 8 brand-new novels every month as they come off the presses. Bill me at the low price of $1.75 each ($1.95 in Canada)—a 11% saving off the retail price. There are no shipping, handling or other hidden costs. There is no minimum number of books I must purchase. I can always return a shipment and cancel at any time. Even if I never buy another book from Harlequin, the 4 free novels and the surprise gift are mine to keep forever.

Name   (PLEASE PRINT)

Address   Apt. No.

City   State/Prov.   Zip/Postal Code

This offer is limited to one order per household and not valid to present subscribers. Price is subject to change.   DOP–SUB–1

PASSIONATE!
CAPTIVATING!
SOPHISTICATED!

Harlequin Presents...

The favorite fiction of women the world over!

Beautiful contemporary romances that touch every emotion of a woman's heart— passion and joy, jealousy and heartache... but most of all...love.

Fascinating settings in the exotic reaches of the world— from the bustle of an international capital to the paradise of a tropical island.

All this and much, much more in the pages of

Harlequin Presents...

Wherever paperback books are sold, or through
Harlequin Reader Service

In the U.S.	In Canada
2504 West Southern Avenue	P.O. Box 2800, Postal Station A
Tempe, AZ 85282	5170 Yonge Street
	Willowdale, Ontario M2N 6J3

No one touches the heart of a woman quite like Harlequin!

P-111